NATIONAL BESTSELLING AUTHOR

MYUNIQUE C. GREEN

# MIDNIGHT TEMPO

Print Edition ISBN: 978-1-105-95884-7

Produced by iWriteBooks Publishing.
iWriteBooksPub.com
MyuniqueGreen.com

## CONNECT WITH MYUNIQUE

Amazon

Goodreads

Blog

# PROLOGUE

Long before Miami pulsed to the heartbeat of bass and neon, there was another kind of music beneath the world. A rhythm older than blood. A sound that could make the ocean rise, the stars falter, the living tremble.

They called it the *Prime Note.*

It was not a song, but a law — the first vibration to shape creation. When it split, the immortal world fractured with it, birthing seven Houses, each bound to one of the primal senses.

*The House of Blood claimed the body.*

*The House of Bone, memory.*

*The House of Smoke, illusion.*

*The House of Flame, desire.*

*The House of Shadow, fear.*

*The House of Silence, control.*

*And the House of Sound—resonance itself.*

Sound was the first to rebel.

Born from the sirens who once ruled the deep, the House of Sound learned early that hunger didn't always have to bleed. Their voices could fill the emptiness left behind by eternity. They fed not on flesh, but on feeling — drawing sustenance from the frequencies that pulsed through emotion: laughter, rage, lust, awe. To feed was to perform. To live was to vibrate.

For centuries, their power shaped empires. Their songs started wars and ended them. Their choirs were worshiped as gods and feared as devils. But as mortal cities rose from the ruins of myth, Sound traded ocean and altar for stage and skyline. The sirens of old became producers, musicians, DJs—immortals hiding in plain sight, feeding on crowds too euphoric to care.

And as Sound grew louder, Silence grew jealous.

The House of Silence was born from the aftermath of noise—vampires who learned to feed not on life, but on absence. They believed stillness was perfection, that silence was purity. To them, Sound's chaos was sin. Their war began the moment the first siren voice shattered a Silent's meditative calm. It has never truly ended.

But time has a way of remixing everything.

Now, in the 21st century, the Houses live like shadows behind celebrity. They rule through industries instead of thrones—politics, luxury, art, war. Their ancient treaties are held together by secrecy and threat. And at the center of it all, under the pulse of South Beach and the hum of sleepless clubs, the Prime Note sleeps, waiting for someone reckless enough to play it again.

They say Miami's heartbeat never stops. They're right. It just has teeth.

And tonight, in the heart of that restless city, a woman named Nyla Voss stands behind a turntable that's older than it looks, her fingers gliding over the sliders like prayer. Her bloodline traces back to the first siren who dared to sing above the waves. Her music can feed a crowd or kill one.

Each night, her mixes ripple through mortals and immortals alike, pulling emotion into sound, sound into hunger. Every bass drop is a pulse of power. Every cheer, a taste of life.

But lately, something inside her set has changed. Beneath the rhythm, under the glamour, she hears another frequency. A voice from the dark whispering through her speakers. And when it wakes, the world will either sing… or fall silent forever.

# I

The night started like a secret the city couldn't keep.

Miami's ocean-salted heat pressed against glass and steel, sliding into every open door on South Beach until it found the one place built to swallow it whole. Midnight Tempo glowed like a heartbeat on the corner—neon in fuchsia and electric blue, light pouring across the sidewalk in glossy sheets. Palms outside shook like metronomes in a coastal breath. Cameras flashed. A hundred perfumes braided themselves with rum and citrus and something copper-sweet beneath the sparkle. Inside, the air tasted like promise and trouble.

The DJ booth towered over it all, a glittering altar. And at the center of that altar, framed by LED ribs and a halo of moving light, stood Nyla Voss.

Omniscience had a favorite angle tonight—the way her sequins threw stars across the room with every turn of her shoulders, the way the crowd leaned toward her without realizing their bodies were asking for permission. She gave it with a smile. She always did. Her hair, cut close on the sides and billowing soft up top, caught the light, blowing a pale-gold sheen with every nod. Curves for days. Posture like the city owed her a thank-you. She lifted one hand, and the room held its breath because Nyla had taught Miami how to breathe on her count.

"Good evening, you beautiful sinners," she said into the mic, voice velvet over steel.

Cheering erupted, not polite, not restrained—an instant boil. Couples pressed closer. Friends abandoned their sawed-off plans for tomorrow morning. Someone's birthday sash slid sideways as she climbed onto a banquette. The club's logo—a sliced crescent moon over a vinyl groove—swept the ceiling in slow, liquid arcs.

Nyla touched the first slider and let a low sub-bass curl up from the floorboards, a pressure you felt in your ribs before your mind noticed it was music. She layered a clipped hi-hat over it, then a synth line that glittered like champagne poured over ice. The mix drifted out, clean and bright, and the crowd began to move with an audible thrill that wasn't quite a shout. Then she dropped the beat—an eruption so precise that glasses in the VIP nook shivered.

Bodies answered. *They always did.*

The House of Sound had learned, long before lasers and smoke cannons, that people didn't come to clubs to forget. They came to choose what they remembered in the morning. Nyla gave them selections—moments cut like diamonds—first chorus kissing second verse, bridge snapping into a breakdown, hand on waist at just the right second, a grin thrown over a shoulder followed by the absolute certainty you'd never be lonely again if you could just keep moving like this.

In the balcony, a tourist couple from Milwaukee who had never stayed out past midnight found that their complaints about airline seats dissolved into a plan to return every year. Two bartenders set a dance-off behind the counter while still hitting every order. A bachelorette squad shrieked at nothing in particular and everything at once. Security exchanged a look that said they'd seen worse and loved better, and tonight might be both.

Nyla fed them joy and took a fraction back. That was the beauty of resonance: it wasn't theft, not the way blood was. It was exchange. You pour your feeling into the air, she siphons off the charge. Everybody leaves a little lighter. Everybody comes back wanting more.

A young man with a camera around his neck pointed his lens up at the booth. He had the posture of someone who was used to staying near walls. Tonight, he'd wandered closer. When Nyla caught him in her view, she gave him a wink that knocked a few years off his slouch. He snapped three shots, lowered the camera, and laughed at himself like a kid caught peeking through a keyhole. Nyla turned a dial with two fingers and rode the cheer his laugh raised. The sound slid into her bones and sizzled—the good kind. The kind she could hold.

"Run it back," a voice shouted from the front rail.

"Patient," Nyla said, lips at the mic, smile turned sideways, full of suggestion. "You'll get your dessert."

The percussion climbed. She teased the crowd with a feathered vocal sample—just a taste, a breath, then gone—and the floor groaned like a wooden ship daring a wave to be bigger. Heat rolled up from bodies in motion, fogging the cool air pumped through the ducts.

A woman in a silver dress touched her own throat and felt the tremor there; she'd tell her group chat later that the music hit a spot no one had named for her yet. A trio of finance bros who had practiced their indifference all evening abandoned it at the first drop that collapsed perfectly into silence then flared. A middle-aged couple with matching bracelets danced the way they hadn't since they met, when the radio had played their favorite song three times an hour by accident.

Nyla watched all of it without looking like she was watching. Her hands moved, a conductor making new weather. Her grin wasn't a promise. It was a guarantee. The crowd thought they made the night. She knew she did.

"Drink water," she said into the mic between transitions. "Hydration is hot."

The laugh that rose had texture—playful, fond, a little shameless. She drank it in and let it ride her spine like a sparkler. The House had an old word for that sensation, for the way a thousand small feelings gathered into power. Nyla didn't bother using the old word. In Miami, you just called it the mix.

She layered in a sample of conga slaps and let them peal against a sun-baked synth, then undercut the whole thing with a bass that walked with extra hip. In the corner, a boy in a bucket hat rolled his neck until his friends screamed the kind of scream that starts fights in other places and starts choreography here. He laughed and folded into a glide. Nyla smiled, pulled him forward like a tide. She didn't need eye contact. Sound did the work.

At the back of the room, a man in a crisp linen shirt stood still. Not stubborn-still. Not bored. Just… centered. He studied the crowd, not the way tourists did—the hungry survey of who to brag to later—but the way techs and architects did, mapping loads and stress points. He watched the floor flex under stampeding feet. He watched the edges, where movement started. He watched the DJ's hands.

He didn't blink much.

Nyla saw him in a flash—her gaze met his and slid, as though her line of sight had hit glass. He didn't look away. He didn't smirk or frown. Just the slightest nod, like he'd been taking notes and the notes agreed with her. She filed him as interesting and let the next loop swallow her curiosity.

"Midnight Tempo," she said, cutting the volume just enough to make the room lean forward. "You're pretty. Let's get messy."

Lights flared. The ceiling's LED ribs pulsed in waves that rippled down the length of the bar. She killed the bass for a heartbeat, then slammed it back in. A dozen glasses chimed in answer. Somewhere on the floor, a button popped from a shirt, two strangers laughed at the same instant, and a woman who had promised herself she'd leave at one stayed, because a song she hadn't heard in years slid under Nyla's hand and became a summer she'd lost and just found again.

A slick-haired promoter in the VIP area tried to wave her attention his way. Nyla let him wait, then gave him the smallest nod that said: I see you, and you can live with that. He melted.

She loved them all a little. It made the feed clean.

The first swell of trouble arrived quietly, the way static crawls along a radio dial just before the station changes. Nyla adjusted a filter and felt the resonance pull against her wrist like a fish testing line. Not a snap, not even a hard tug—just tension where there shouldn't be. She frowned, barely. No one saw.

She eased the high end down and lifted the low, cushioning the room in velvet. The floor responded with a collective shiver of pleasure. The tension slackened.

Good girl, she told the system with a touch. Behave.

At the far end of the bar, Marisol—club manager, lipstick lethal—watched Nyla over the rim of a coupe glass. Marisol had a six-sense for crowd weather, the kind of vision that could predict a spill before the glass tipped. She saw the micro-frown. She pressed her mouth into a line and slid her phone free without taking her gaze off the booth, thumbs moving: You good?

Nyla didn't glance at her phone. She gave the room a sing-song "don't worry" with a three-note keyboard flourish and rode the crowd's answering cheer until it poured back into her. It steadied the tiny flicker under her sternum.

She loved this—this being a lighthouse and a storm at once.

Phone screens rose, capturing her silhouette framed in violet haze, the sequined top flashing like a constellation map every time she turned. A club kid with glitter-dusted cheeks wept happy tears into a friend's shoulder because the bridge she loved hit exactly right and no one told her that would happen tonight; it did, and it changed something small and important inside her.

Nyla heard the tear catch in the kid's breath, tasted the saline brightness as if it dissolved on her tongue. She soaked it in. The power hummed—that word out of bounds for most artists, but in the House, it meant the body had found the frequency it was born for. She wouldn't call it that aloud tonight. Some words sounded like superstition if you hadn't stood on a rocky coast and learned them under a moon that never set.

She rode the next transition with a grin that walked the line between tease and dare. Three men along the rail angled their bodies like sundials pointing at her. Two women at the center nodded in agreement at something without exchanging a single sentence. Someone near the back filmed in vertical even though he knew horizontal looked better. That was fine; when he watched it tomorrow morning, the clip would still make his chest tighten.

"Pull up," someone yelled, a prayer disguised as a request.

"Ask nicely," Nyla said, hand hovering over the cutoff.

"Please!"

"There we go." She cut the bass, waited one beat, two—let the crowd's sound pile into her palms like a gift—then slammed the drop harder than before.

That's when she felt the glitch again, needle-small and sneaky, sliding between layers.

The sub-bass stuttered where it should have stayed smooth. Not a failure, just a misstep. The crowd heard it and loved it, because surprise makes memory. Nyla felt it and did not love it—not when she could feel the misstep pull a thread of energy from her center without offering anything back. She skimmed the filters left and right, landed the line, tied it off. The floor shivered with relief.

"Easy," she breathed—more to the system than the crowd, more to herself than either.

The man in linen didn't clap, didn't flick his chin. He just watched her choose a new path through the next four bars like someone who had built roadways and enjoyed seeing a brilliant driver take a curve better than the blueprint expected.

Omniscience dips in and out of individual skulls for fun; it brushed his and found cool lakes. Silence inside him made its own shape. Not hollow—just ordered. The kind of quiet that knows its edge and defends it. Useful. Dangerous. Nyla's attention skated across him again, filed him in a folder she labeled Later without knowing why.

"Last call for common sense," Marisol announced from the bar, voice sugary with warning. "Meaning none."

Laughter lifted. The room grew louder in a way that wasn't about decibels—it was permission. Permission has a sound. Nyla twisted that permission into a coil and let it spring across the dance floor. People leapt with it, like a wave was coming and they had surfboards made of bone.

The neon at the club's rear exit blinked twice and steadied. A bouncer paused, then shook his head; faulty ballast. He touched his ear, checked with Ava at the door, got a thumbs-up. Business as usual. Outside, the crush of waiting bodies had formed a little festival of impatience—selfies taken in the day's last heat, stilettos clicking a chorus, someone in a feather jacket convincing his boyfriend that, yes, they'd get in; he had a guy. Inside, a celebrity who wasn't supposed to be there ducked behind a plant and pretended the plant helped.

Nyla layered in a vocal run from a '90s deep cut and tasted the room's collective joy swell. She breathed it, drew it through her like a cord that connected each chest to her hands. Her pupils dilated. Her pulse slowed. This was the good feed, the kind that left everyone glossy and unafraid. The sequins tracing her waist flashed as she swayed.

A college girl near the front blinked too fast and reached for her friend's shoulder. "I'm fine," she said, then, "I swear," then, "Okay, maybe I need—"

Nyla saw it even before Security did: an edge of bliss tipping toward overload. She pulled the high end down another hair's breadth, bounced the low frequency two ticks softer. The room sighed. The girl breathed. Her friend kissed her forehead like a seal over a love letter. A bartender slipped a water over the rail, muscle memory and compassion welded together.

"Good save," Marisol murmured into her own mic from the bar, pitched just to Nyla's monitors.

"Always," Nyla murmured back.

Someone behind Nyla lifted a phone to grab a close shot. She didn't mind being the content of other people's nights. Let them keep a piece. They'd come back for the rest.

A runner in a satin bomber jacket dashed up the stairs to the booth and handed off a fresh towel and a glass with lime. "From Ava," the runner shouted over the beat. "Said you looked too good to sweat, and it made her mad."

"Tell Ava I love her and she's wrong," Nyla shouted back, dabbing her neck with the towel. "Sweat's a flex."

The runner beamed and vanished.

On the floor, a duo whose first date had been scheduled to end at an hour ago forgot that schedules existed. A man in a coral sport coat proposed a very temporary marriage of convenience to a stranger who laughed and almost said yes. A woman whose divorce had finalized that afternoon climbed onto the stage left riser and danced like a witness for herself.

Nyla fed. The House took note. Invisible ledgers updated. Somewhere in a mirrored office across town, Maestra Ardelia glanced at a display of moving bars and thought, as she often did on nights like this: Let her have it. She's earned the sun she makes.

But omniscience knows that even generosity can be a leash.

At 1:17, Nyla pivoted into a blend that always leveled the place—a classic Miami bass line tucked beneath a French disco charm with an Afro-Caribbean drum figure tapped into the corners. The dance floor rose as one organism and shouted the unsayable: that nights like this last forever. They do not, but it feels true, and that's all resonance needs to gorge itself.

The linen-shirt watcher stepped one foot forward, placing himself directly beneath the booth's left monitor, as if testing a boundary. He rested his palm on the railing, feeling the wooden grain shake. He mouthed a number—BPM, calculated—then nodded. He looked up at Nyla again. The look did not ask. It confirmed.

She gave him an eyebrow that said: I know exactly what I'm doing.

He returned a fractional smile, one that never made it to his eyes.

In the second row of the floor, a tall woman with a shaved head and tattooed vines trailing her neck lifted her hands and closed her eyes. Nyla bled a little more high end into the mix and watched the woman's shoulders relax. Nyla felt the relief pour through the cord and into her own chest. She didn't need blood. She needed this: relief given flesh.

The glitch returned, sudden and greedy.

It came in on the end of a snare—an extra shimmer that wasn't hers, thin as foil and wrong in the way a too-sweet drink turns your stomach halfway through. Nyla flinched, the barest rake of her mouth. The feed surged and then snagged; for a hair of a second, she took in nothing, and the nothing felt cold.

She cut mids by reflex, swore under her breath, and set her hands steadier. Her cue points were muscle memory and faith, her board a living thing that demanded the exact touch it had always loved. She gave it. The snag loosened. The room, none the wiser, roared as she flowed into the chorus from a summer that smelled like sunscreen and recklessness.

Marisol's eyes found her. Question. Nyla gave a small nod: handled.

The linen man's mouth barely moved. He had noticed. Not the crowd; not the bar; him. His brow folded by one degree. He slid his hand off the railing and tucked both hands into his pockets like a polite guest lowering his voice in a library where he did not belong.

Nyla rolled the next track in and pasted a grin over a new sliver of worry. If something in her board or chain was off, she'd burn it after last call. If something in her was off—

No. Later.

"Alright, saints and sinners," she said, tilting the mic. "Let's play favorites."

Favorites. The crowd's sound brightened—all those tiny, private jukeboxes inside their ribs powering up at once. She let the anticipation simmer. Anticipation fed beautifully—clean, sunlit, open.

She teased the opening notes of a hit with a piano lick that made bartenders dance, then twisted the sample into a fresh pattern that made the entire balcony whine and then cheer when the chorus arrived on time anyway. Joy rose like steam. Nyla laid her palm over the fader and felt the warmth soak in.

For a moment, it felt like the early years again, before other Houses had learned her name, before labels called and streaming counts tried to put her in a box with a label and a price. For a moment, it was just her and a city open like a new diary, willing to believe she could write every page.

She caught the camera-kid's eye again. He'd drifted closer, sweat beading on his forehead, grin wide. He lifted his camera, and this time when he took the shot, he didn't look at the screen to check it. He knew it would be good because the moment was. He lowered the camera and pressed a hand to his sternum, surprised by his own chest.

"Breathe," Nyla mouthed to him.

He nodded, inhaled, exhaled. The gratitude that shimmered in his eyes slid into Nyla like a sip of cold water. She closed her eyes. Let it settle. Let it power the next measure.

Up in the lighting rig, the techs who called themselves Sky Pirates swung one spotlight into a lazy orbit that landed on the disco ball and sent a million tiny planets across the bodies below. The room gasped—sincere, childlike—and then laughed at itself for gasping. Nyla rode the laugh. Laughter fed like champagne: quick to the head, quick to the heart.

The linen man stepped sideways, then forward again, calibrating. He touched the monitor stand; wood and metal buzzed beneath his palm. He shut his eyes for a beat and listened with his bones. Something passed over his face, a realization slid into place with no fanfare. He opened his eyes and looked back at Nyla a third time. The look was fiercer now, and kinder. This, the look said, is dangerous.

Nyla couldn't name why the caution warmed her. Maybe because it wasn't possessive. Maybe because it wasn't fear. It was the kind of caution you offer a fighter before a match: brilliant, you're brilliant, please don't miss the blade. She rolled her neck, shook out her shoulders, and smiled like trouble.

At 1:39, a fan near the front rail—a woman in a sunset-orange slip with barre-strong calves—lifted both arms and tilted her head back to take in the light. Her mouth opened on a sound lost to the music. Her knees didn't buckle so much as disagree with her. She swayed.

Nyla saw it first. She always did.

She dipped the master volume by a sliver—barely enough for the ears, but enough to let breath back in. She eased the gain on the left deck down, stretched a bar into two, giving bodies time to regulate. The woman blinked and steadied, a hand catching the rail. Security moved in with practiced nonchalance, offering water like an in-joke. The woman drank, nodded a thousand times, laughed at herself, then raised the bottle to Nyla in salute.

Nyla's shoulders softened. The feed slid sweet again.

She leaned into the mic. "Hey, check in with your people. We good?"

A wave of thumbs-ups and yeses rolled through the room. A few sarcastic salutes. A middle finger tossed lovingly from a guy whose friends immediately shoved his head. The energy lifted like a kite taking a gust.

Omniscience, fond of little truths, skimmed the surface of the city beyond the doors: yachts with LED undersides pushing showers of light along dark water; 24-hour diners frying eggs nobody needed; a rooftop two streets over where a girl in a glitter dress took off her shoes and realized she could stand taller barefoot; a priest in Little Havana turning a cup slowly in his hands, fighting sleep;

a cop on the causeway who had picked the wrong night to be decent; a Council aide checking a feed that plotted the night's frequencies on a graph only three people knew how to read. Threads everywhere, tugged by the same unseen hand.

Inside Midnight Tempo, the unseen hand belonged to Nyla.

She let a salsa horn line peek in and out, taunting, then bent it into a trap cadence that should have annoyed purists and instead made purists throw their hands up and yell even louder. Her mind worked like a chess board stacked on a dance floor: move here, laugh there, breathe here, touch now. She was show and chef and Spell-maker, pouring people into a mold called Yes.

The glitch hit again. Not random this time. Intent.

It curled like foil under flame, thin and bright, and sliced between layers with the precision of a blade. Nyla's fingers stilled. Every hair along her forearm lifted. The feed… stuttered. The crowd kept dancing, never noticing the half-second void where Nyla took in nothing and felt a cold that didn't belong to Florida touch her lungs.

She set her jaw. She nudged the crossfader and split the signal, isolating the trouble frequency. She dragged it down like pulling a kite out of a tangle. The room didn't realize they were in a twitch of danger, because the danger was lovelier than fear: joy sharpened until it cut.

Marisol saw the set of Nyla's shoulders and swore under her breath. She flagged a tech. "Eyes on power. Now."

Ava at the door replied in her channel, "We're green across."

"Doesn't feel green," Marisol said.

"Then it's not the board," Ava said, quiet now.

Nyla landed the correction like a gymnast who refuses to wobble, and the crowd erupted the way crowds do when the landing looks effortless. She took their praise, distributed it through her limbs, and forced the tremor in her hands to vanish.

A boy on his third gin soda dropped to one knee to tie his shoe and decided, while he was down there, to confess to the man next to him that he liked boys. The man smiled and said, "Cool. Me too." Nyla felt that tiny, huge shift slide up to her booth like a ripple. She swallowed it, grateful. It tasted like a light turned on in a room that had been dark for years.

The linen man's hands were back on the railing. He mouthed another number, lower this time. He closed his eyes again, as if listening for where the building held its breath. He wasn't dancing. But something inside him was moving—an engine engaging.

He stepped left. Security slid an inch. Not an issue. Not yet.

Nyla leaned forward, close enough to the mic that her lip gloss touched the metal. "Alright," she said. "We're going to push."

A cheer built with no ceiling.

She slammed a double-time bridge into place. The floor rose and scattered like confetti, then gathered itself and jumped together. The light techs chased white across the ceiling and then drowned the place in pink. Someone in the corner had a small flag in their pocket for no reason except that it felt right, and they waved it because the song told them to be larger than their square footage.

Nyla threw her head back. The feed surged.

There—something in that surge pulled against her, like a fish diving when you expected it to leap. For a microsecond, she saw not the crowd, not the booth, but a room of mirrors where sound bent into shapes older than speakers. The old voices—the ones the House kept archived in grooves and code—rose, as if they'd been invited without her consent. Not loud. Not full. Just a trace, a hallway far away. The notes were sweet and terrible.

The linen man opened his eyes at the exact second Nyla's breath hitched. He didn't know the archives. He didn't know the siren reels. He knew physics and failure and the sound of wood about to break. He moved.

He stepped beneath the stairs to the booth and took them two at a time, not sprinting, but with that steady, inevitable speed that gets there faster than panic ever does. Security missed him for two beats because they were watching a scuffle at the bar that turned out to be friends playing, and because his posture said worker, not problem. By the time Ava's voice hit the channel—"Linen shirt heading up"—he was already at the half-landing, and by the time a guard reached for him, he'd lifted both hands, palms open, and said, "Sound," which could be anything and everything in this building.

Nyla saw him at the top of the stairs, three steps from her booth, and something inside her—some ancient tripwire that belonged to a queen who had once stood on a cliff and sang—snapped into an alert so fierce she could taste iron.

He stopped before the final step, hands still open. Not a threat posture. Not submissive either. A collaborative refusal to scare her.

"Your left deck," he said, voice calm, carrying with the precision of a stage whisper that was not a whisper at all. "It's catching a reflection from your own output. Phase offset."

"Cute," Nyla said without looking away from her board. "So are you. Go dance. I got it."

"You do," he said, with a nod that took her skill as fact. "But the room doesn't. You'll steer it, but the feedback will keep tasting you."

He said tasting like a person who didn't know he'd picked the exact wrong and right word.

Nyla lifted her chin. "You a tech?"

"Engineer."

"Oh, we got a real one," she said, grin edged, hands still flying. "What's your name, real one?"

"Kian."

"Okay, Kian," she said, drawing the vowels out like a lesson. "If you touch this board, I will end you and make it look poetic."

"I won't touch your board," he said. His gaze flicked to the left monitor, to a tiny LED readout most eyes would dismiss. He looked back at her. "But if you step on that pedal, you'll catch yourself again."

Nyla's eyes flicked to the pedal—small and black, hidden by the stand. She hadn't stepped on it all night. She never toggled it during blends; it lived there for a very specific trick she sometimes pulled in the last half hour when the city needed to leave floating. It was not on.

"It's not engaged," she said.

"Someone thinks it is," Kian said, and tilted his head toward the rig. "Audio's getting told a lie."

The word lie had its own shadow. It slid under her skin and found old bones.

"Marisol," Nyla said into her inner mic, which Kian could not hear. "Check pedal feed."

Marisol didn't ask why. "On it." A tech scrambled, hands like live wire over snake-cabled guts. He found the loop and grimaced. "Somebody mirrored the out."

"Fix it," Marisol said.

"I am. Stop making me nervous."

"You were born nervous."

"True."

Nyla watched Kian while she slid the low down half a tick and brought in a handclap from a sample that belonged to a garage in London before she'd been born. Kian's face didn't tremble. It didn't sweat. He stood in sound like he was standing in wind—calculating lift and drag. He looked at her not the way fans did, not the way rivals did. He looked at her like a colleague in a field neither of them would admit on paper.

"Don't worry," she said, because she said it to everybody and meant it every time. "I don't break."

"I can see that," Kian said. "But it might try you."

"Everything tries me." She smiled, then leaned into the mic for the crowd. "Who said we could keep going?"

The roar made the ceiling shake.

"Cool." She cut the track, left a single, clean drum running, then clapped into the mic, three times, off the grid by just enough to feel human. The room clapped back on instinct. She grinned. "There we go. Now we're in the same house."

Kian's eyes narrowed, just a little. He felt it—the way she gathered them and tuned them and took from them and gave back more. He felt the exchange like static raising along the length of his forearms. He did not step back.

"Don't lean on that left," he said, casual, as if they were talking over a kitchen island and not over an ocean. "It's still ghosting. You'll be pulling from yourself."

"Thought you said you wouldn't touch my board."

"I'm not touching your board," he said, a hint of humor at last. "I'm touching your ego."

She laughed, hard and delighted, and the crowd thought it was for them. In a way, it was.

"Okay, Kian," she said. "Stay. Watch me work."

"I am," he said.

She slid into a new blend that required absolute trust in her hands and none in the left output. She rerouted in her head and then in the hardware, rolling her main through the center and giving the room a fresh channel that felt like a door opening. The glitch scratched at the frame and then sulked away. The feed came in sweet and full again. Nyla drank it down and let it wash through her veins like a promise kept.

Kian felt the shift in the wood under his palms. He nodded once—respect, unadorned.

"Good call," Nyla said without looking at him.

"Yours," he said.

"Mm. Shared," she said, and she didn't share credit as a habit. It felt... pleasurable. Strange.

He started to step back down the stairs.

"Wait," she said, eyes still on her gear. "You working tonight?"

"Not here."

"Somewhere?"

"Consulting."

"That where you learned to say nothing while saying a lot?"

"Pretty much."

"Cute," she said again, but the word didn't have claws in it now. "If you break my board with your thoughts, I'll make you fix it with your hands."

"I don't break things I like," he said.

Nyla looked up at that. The remark wasn't a flirt. It rested on an honesty she didn't get often from the drunk, the thirsty, or the immortal. It made a small, bright point in the middle of the noise.

"Then don't go far," she said.

He nodded, gave the pedals one final glance like a surgeon checking a heartbeat, and moved back down into the crowd. Security parted just enough to allow it, then filled the space. He vanished near the bar's end, swallowed by light.

Nyla rode the win.

She pushed the tempo a hair and grinned as the room lifted with her. The feed ripped through her now, generous and clean. She let her hips move, a slow, decisively sensual sway that sent shockwaves of desire out like pebbles into water. Heads turned. Lower lips caught between teeth. A dozen micro-crushes were born and would die fondly tomorrow.

"Y'all are pretty," she said. "Let's do one more ugly-pretty and then I'll let you breathe."

They booed at breathe, because it suggested leaving, and then cheered because they knew she never kept her promises when it came to stopping. She laughed, pure sunlight, and poured them a track built for the exact geometry of their bodies. It fit like new denim and old love.

For five minutes, nothing existed but bass and sweat, glitter and heat, taste of lime and lip gloss, whir of a camera lens, click of a heel, scrape of a barstool pulled closer, the thud of a hand on a friend's back, the kiss of a stranger who wasn't one anymore, and a goddess at a booth pulling energy up through the floorboards as if lifting a city out of the sea by hand.

At 1:52, when she should have felt sated—full up and glowing—she felt instead the faintest hollowness, like a mouthful of air where there should have been water. She masked it. She always would. She lifted both hands, and the room shouted like it was their idea.

"Miami," she called, voice dripping sugar and threat. "One more."

They begged. They roared. They loved her enough to break themselves for her, and she would never ask it. She set a final song free, one designed to let people leave feeling taller than the doorframe. It moved, and so did they.

Omniscience leaned down to the booth, placed a hand between Nyla's shoulder blades, and said the thing only a few would admit at dawn: the night gives, but it keeps a ledger. Somewhere on that ledger, a thin line in a different color had appeared, a credit or a debt, unclear. She would find out soon enough.

For now, she was the pulse and the cure. For now, she was the city's favorite sin dressed up as salvation. For now, she was Nyla Voss: charm turned blade, wit turned sugar, predator turned saint, saint turned storm. And whether the room understood the exact magic or not didn't matter. They felt it. And she fed.

# II

Miami at four a.m. wore its afterglow like lipstick smeared on the edge of a glass—still bright, a little dangerous, ready to swear it hadn't been out all night. Sea air threaded through alleys, bringing salt and the faint iron-tinge you only noticed when the streets emptied. Nyla drove with the windows cracked, the city's pulse running cool over her skin. Sequins had been traded for a graphite tracksuit that caught no light and a hood that framed the pale blaze of her hair. Her skin kept the sheen that club mirrors adored, but the hunger underneath had sharpened since she killed the booth lights. Glitter never lasted. Appetite did.

Arista House Records looked asleep in the front—turquoise sign low, lobby plants resting like they believed in bedtime. The real entrance waited out back: a steel door with a brass plate that claimed Adagio & Co. to anyone who didn't know better, a plate that warmed under her palm like skin. The scan kissed her hand and cooled. Locks unlatched in a quick sequence that sounded like a room taking a polite breath before company.

The hallway inside smelled of pine cleaner, cold metal, and something copper-bright the building never tried too hard to hide. Framed "records" lined the wall; up close, the grooves weren't audio at all but sigils pressed to channel and store. A vintage reel-to-reel gleamed inside a glass case like a reliquary. LED strips ran low along the baseboards instead of overhead—the House preferred light that didn't cast judgments.

Marisol stood in the break room doorway with a glass vial between two fingers. Her lipstick was still lethal; her bun hadn't moved since midnight. She looked rested in the way night creatures did—still, composed, no apologies about it.

"Back entrance was clean," she said, handing Nyla the vial.

Nyla lifted the vial marked O-negative, the deep red glinting beneath the studio lights. To anyone else, it might look like blood, but the House of Sound had moved past such crude indulgences. This was resonance concentrate—a synthetic feed crafted from captured frequencies of human emotion: laughter, heartbreak, desire, and pain distilled into liquid form.

"Front?" Nyla asked, even as she unstopped the vial and let the scent unfurl.

"Two tourists asking if our 'indie label' is hiring interns. I gave them a QR code for nowhere."

When she tilted it to her lips, she wasn't tasting iron; she was tasting memory—the trace of a crowd's joy, bottled and humming softly as it slid down her throat.

Marisol watched, assessing for color and cadence, the way she always did. "Better?"

The color only mimicked blood, a reminder of what their kind had once been before they learned to feed through feeling instead of flesh. "Better," Nyla said. "I kept it clean at the club. A few grazes, nothing ugly."

Ardelia called it progress. Nyla called it poetry. Every performance was another feast, every vibration a heartbeat waiting to be devoured. She held it on her tongue for a second, then swallowed and felt the heat unfurl low, steady, measured. Not a binge, a correction.

"Your board tried to flirt with itself. I saw the clip."

"It tried to pull me back through my own signal. I don't do loop-de-loops."

"Ardelia's in A," Marisol said. "She didn't call it an emergency. She did call it 'now.' That tone."

"That tone," Nyla echoed, and the corner of her mouth twitched. The Maestra didn't need volume to command. She had other tools.

They crossed the corridor filled with quiet trophies—the kind that didn't clink—into Studio A, where the air felt wrapped, intentional. The live room held its breath like a choir waiting for a downbeat. In the control room, the console glowed with a low constellation of LEDs. Two large monitors, silent and watchful. Baffles that looked like sculpture until they did their job. A velvet cover draped half off the piano's back as if someone had left mid-song promising they'd return.

Maestra Ardelia sat at the heart of it, silk robe the shade of deep wine over a black slip, hair set into a crown that didn't need jewels. Her throat carried a fine chain with an antique clasp, old enough to have watched empires change their minds. No rings—she liked her hands free to bless or to bar. The light leaned toward her as if even electricity had manners.

"Enter," Ardelia said. The word held welcome and inventory at once.

Nyla stepped in. The door sealed, and the world outside turned into suggestion. "If I say I missed you, you'll say I'm performing," she drawled, dropping into the engineer's chair like it knew her spine.

"You perform as easily as breathing," Ardelia said, not unkind. "It is one of your gifts and one of your dangers. Sit. Let me look."

Nyla let herself be looked at. The Maestra's eyes moved like artists' fingers—taking a face apart, finding the fault lines, setting the pieces back in a way that worked better than original.

"Good color," Ardelia said. "Pupils clean. Shoulders are pretending not to ache."

"They always pretend," Nyla said. "The set was loud with joy. A proper mess. It fed clean. I took only what the room offered."

"And the snag."

"A ghost return on the left," Nyla said. "A mirrored feed. I rerouted. I had assistance."

"Name," Ardelia said, as if tasting it in advance.

"Kian."

"Surname?" The question wasn't a test; it was policy.

"I didn't ask and he didn't insist."

"That shows sense in both of you." Ardelia let one fingertip graze the console. "He saw what he was looking at?"

"He knew what the room would do if I leaned on wrong. Steady eyes, steady hands, no idiot courage."

"Useful," Ardelia said, with the dry economy she reserved for praise. "We'll return to him. Tell me about the hunger."

Nyla rolled the little glass vial between two knuckles. "Held until the car. The club fed me without biting—joy, relief, little flashes of desire. The good kind. It kept the need in a straight line. But the glitch..." She flexed her hand, remembering that thin cold slice. "It tried to turn me inward. It tasted like me, wrong."

Ardelia's gaze settled. "Say the lesson."

"If I drink myself, I lose the edge between us and them. Then I can't tell where the City ends and my throat begins. And I can't be trusted to stop."

"Good." The Maestra's mouth warmed, which meant she approved and remembered why approval mattered. "You keep your covenants in public because you practice them in private. We are custodians of pulse. You don't let the pulse reach back through the wire and take a bite."

Nyla's smile tilted. "You always say it better than I do."

"I say it older," Ardelia answered. "Older isn't better. It is, however, harder to argue with. House business." She shifted in her chair, the silk whispering secrets to itself. "The Silence has been busy."

Nyla had felt the edge of that even before the text—moods slipping strange during the last bars of nights she didn't play, rooftop parties with sound that made the sky feel weighty instead of infinite. Flyers for events that looked minimal but felt hungry. People leaving clubs satisfied in the mouth and empty behind the eyes.

"How close?" she asked.

"Close enough to smell," Ardelia said. "They're testing rooftops again, Brickell and a spot in the Grove—quiet invitations, quiet exits. They call it peace. They mean quiet lungs. We like lungs noisy."

"They collect." Nyla didn't spit the word, but she didn't make it gentle. "Take breaths without leaving kisses."

"Accurate enough," Ardelia said. "They're not monsters in their own story. They never are. They have rules. So do we. Ours are older."

"Older and popular," Nyla said. "I watched a girl tonight receive the right bridge at the right time and remember the piece of herself she put away in ninth grade. She'll keep that. Silence can't offer her that."

"They can offer safety from sharp edges," Ardelia said. "And you—" a small smile "—you love sharp edges."

"I love clean lines," Nyla corrected, and Ardelia's eyes laughed.

"We will not be reactive. We will be excellent," the Maestra said. "Your name rose on their ledgers tonight. That doesn't worry me. It does make me careful."

"The House knows my name already," Nyla said. "So does the City."

"They know your stage name," Ardelia said. "Silence keeps another index." She tipped her head toward the isolation booth. "Before we talk assignments, give me a run. I'd like to hear where the snag bit and whether it left teeth."

Nyla stood, shook the weight from her arms, and stepped into the booth. The door closed with that soft expensive kiss. Headphones on, cable secure. The booth's air felt disciplined. Here, breath itself had posture.

Ardelia's voice came through clear. "Start with breath. No pitch, just tone. Find your line."

Nyla let air stream out until it caught and held, a column without words. The studio caught it and returned the taste: mint-cool over heat, saline under metal, the faintest sweetness that made a body think of the inside of a wrist. She shaped that column thinner, then widened it hair by hair. The old training settled in her bones—before clubs and neon and late-night radio hits, there had been stone rooms and closed mouths and learning how to turn want into a tool.

"Good," Ardelia said. "Left gain at two hairs. Say when you feel the wobble."

"Now," Nyla said, the instant that bright insincere shimmer slid in.

"You're not slow," another voice observed—not cutting, simply true.

Kian stepped into the control room with a small case tucked under one arm, in slate again, sleeves rolled. Linen had been traded for something that could kneel under a console without hating him. He didn't fill the doorway; he didn't try. He took the room in the glance of someone who had measured rooms his whole life.

"Mr. Kian," Ardelia said, acknowledging without ceremony. "Thank you for not sleeping."

"I don't like unsolved problems," he said, setting the case on a side table. His eyes flicked to Nyla in the booth, not appraising, not unsure—calibrating. "And I was curious who could bend a crowd like that and still walk out upright."

"Get used to her," Ardelia said. "We'll be paying you to."

Kian's mouth slanted at one corner—the micro-expression of a man who understood humor but saved his laugh for later. "Permission to watch your hands?"

"You can watch," Ardelia said. "You do not touch my board unless I say your name first."

"Understood," he said, and meant it. He moved a stool three feet off the console and sat, respectful angle, attention on the meters, then Nyla, then the corners of the room.

"Again," Ardelia told Nyla.

Nyla rethreaded the tone. Kian listened—not just with ears; with posture, with skin. When the shimmer crept in, his head cocked. "Upper left seam," he said. "Where the panels meet. It's small. Enough to tickle when she widens."

"Agreed," Ardelia said. "Tomorrow we brace it."

"Tonight we notch it," he said. "Left hand, one dB at—ask forgiveness if I'm wrong—three-fifty-eight?"

Ardelia's eyes slid. She considered, then inclined her head. "Your left hand, yes."

He reached, precise. No flourish, no fist. A minimal subtraction, respectful as a bow. "Again," he said to Nyla, voice level.

She widened joy across the line. The false sheen stepped aside as if asked politely and finally heard the please behind the math.

"Better," Kian said.

"Say the actual compliment," Nyla said, and let a smile coat the vowels.

"You make this room feel larger than it is," he said, not trying for poetry, landing there anyway. "And the room likes it."

"Keep him," Nyla told Ardelia.

"I intend to," the Maestra said. "Six weeks to start. Afternoon load tests twice a week. Set lists submitted for major nights. Kian stabilizes your floor and builds you a filter."

"Define filter," Nyla said, though the word had already slid into the part of her mind that loved toys.

"A portable screen that listens before you do," Kian said. He set his case on his lap, opened it to reveal components arranged with affection: coils, tiny drivers, a strip that looked like jewelry and failed to be tacky. "It takes the trash frequencies and bleeds them to ground before they reach your line. Small, subtle, camera-friendly."

Marisol drifted into the doorway with a platter she'd fetched from the cold room: a line of black glass flasks beaded with condensation, each labeled in shorthand, each resting in velvet cutouts. "Say the word 'pendant' at least once, and make it pretty."

"It can be a pendant," Kian said, not missing a beat. "Or a clip for her headphone cable. Or a thin strip under a booth edge. The shape is a negotiation with vanity."

"I don't have vanity," Nyla said on cue.

The room did her the favor of laughing for her.

"Your vanity is a protective charm," Ardelia said. "We keep it polished." She angled her chin at the platter. "Feed."

Nyla stepped out of the booth. The control room air wrapped around her shoulders like a shawl that understood duty. She selected a flask by scent—citrus under copper, Ardelia's preferred blend for post-set stabilization—and slid the straw beneath a canine. The first pull landed like a chord struck true: clarity, heat, relief with no drag behind it. Her spine loosened. The need that had grown teeth on the drive settled into a well-behaved line. Sirens had a thousand ways to misbehave; the House required one—feed with grace.

Kian didn't look away. He didn't stare. He held his gaze the way good medics did—present, unflinching, unfazed. When she capped the flask, he lifted a brow. "Taste profile?"

"Bright," Nyla said. "Ardelia's way of telling me to aim up, not out."

"Accurate," the Maestra said, pleased by the read. "Now the part you don't like."

"Rules," Nyla said, with a sigh she didn't fake. "Go on."

"You do not chase Silence," Ardelia said. "If they send an invitation, it arrives in daylight with etiquette. If they tug at night on a rooftop, you don't look. You let them speak to me in rooms with locks. If anything tastes like you, you cut. I will not say please about that."

"I won't drink my own echo," Nyla said. "I know what that does. It makes the city taste like a mirror, and I'm not in love with my face."

Kian glanced at the console, at the pedal chain, at the far seam of the floor. "I'll trace the liar feed today," he said, using the same word he'd used at the club without apology. "Whoever mirrored it either didn't know what they were doing or knew exactly. Either way, we take it out of your field."

"Language," Ardelia said, but it came with the warmth she reserved for people who made themselves useful. "While you do that, you will remember we have ways of listening deeper than your meters. Ask questions. Ask permission. You'll get both."

Kian nodded once, then shifted his stool an inch closer to the patch bay. He did not reach out. "I want to put a passive coil near her left channel. Not on the board. On the rack. It will tell me when the room feeds back intent, not just sound."

"Intent?" Nyla asked.

"The way the wave behaves when a human room stops acting like wood and people and starts acting like a thing with wants," he said. He didn't glance at Ardelia when he said it. He trusted she already knew.

"She trained you to say that," Nyla said, amused.

"No," Ardelia said. "He taught himself. Men like that are rare. We pay them."

Marisol raised a flask at that. "Amen."

"Do not invoke anyone I owe favors to," Ardelia replied, dry. She turned to Nyla again. "You will do Sunrise Sessions radio for two songs and a smile. You will not let them keep you longer. You will not take samples from their coffee table. You will feed before you go."

Nyla set the flask in its velvet cradle. "I'll send them away charmed and unsure why they agreed to shorter segments."

"Use your siren voice lightly," Ardelia said, and those words carried memory—stone rooms again, low lamps, elders who had burned cities by mistake and taught their heirs not to.

Nyla nodded. The thirst had evened out; the edges of her senses had sharpened into useful. Through the glass, the piano waited with its velvet half-shawl. Guitars slept on their stands. Miami exhaled in the distance as the sky made up its mind.

"Before we let you go," Ardelia said, "there is the matter of introductions."

Nyla turned to Kian fully. "In the booth you watched the meters before my face. That buys you good will. In the club you gave direction without touching. That buys you trust. In this room you will keep both by remembering one thing I'll say only once."

Kian's attention tightened. "I'm listening."

"Do not treat my gift like a trick to be solved," Nyla said. "When it misbehaves, it isn't a broken toaster. It's a sea getting ideas. You read seas. You don't scold them."

He considered that and then nodded, serious as a contract signed in ink that doesn't fade. "I'll build for tides, not toasters."

Ardelia allowed herself a sliver of a smile. "Good. I like the two of you in a sentence."

Marisol slid the platter back toward the cold room. "I'll stock the alley fridge," she said. "Just in case your radio escort gets thirsty ideas."

"Wouldn't be the first," Nyla said. She looked to Ardelia. "Anything else I should pretend to resist?"

"Two more items." The Maestra lifted a finger. "One: if you feel sharp for fun, leave. Bring that here and we will file it down together. Your wit is a weapon; you don't need it to cut allies."

Nyla accepted the check. "Noted."

"Two: if Silence calls your name from a crowd, do nothing. If they use my name, do nothing louder. We choose when we turn. Not them."

Kian made a small note on a pad he'd produced from nowhere. "If she gets pale—"

"You call me," Ardelia said. "If she refuses to cut when her body orders it, you lean to her left ear and speak mine.

It is a key we built a long time ago. She will not like it; it will work; you will not enjoy using it; do it anyway."

"That key exists?" Nyla asked, a little amazed, a little offended, a little impressed.

Ardelia's eyes softened. "I made it when you were newer. I haven't had to use it in years. I would like that streak to continue."

"It will," Nyla said, because saying it made it true more often than not.

The hallway lights dipped an increment toward dawn. Somewhere in the building, the espresso machine cycled a rinse; the scent rose and vanished, more memory than drink. Nyla's tongue tasted copper and citrus and the soft high thread of joy from the club that still wanted to play.

Kian stood, closed his case, and slung it like an instrument. "I'll start with the pedal chain and the rack. Then I'll sweep the subfloor seam. If your schedule allows this afternoon, we can run an edge test."

"I have radio, then a nap with my eyes open," Nyla said. "After, bring whatever jewelry you're pretending is a tool."

"You'll pretend it's jewelry," he said. "I'll pretend it's a tool. We both win."

"Keep the finish matte," Marisol called as she disappeared through the cold-room door. "No glare on camera."

"Understood," Kian said, and his mouth put the smallest curve on the syllable when he looked at Nyla—respect, curiosity, a truce.

Ardelia rose. The robe fell into place like fabric owed her obedience. She stepped close and lifted two fingers to Nyla's jaw, the lightest touch, a check that was more blessing than exam. "You did not lose yourself tonight," she said. "That is the bar. The City will try to make you bigger than your name. Remember it is your name."

Nyla dipped her head, a gesture that would have been a bow if she believed in bowing. "Yes, Maestra."

"Go," Ardelia said. "Be dazzling without being devoured. If Silence breathes near you, breathe louder."

Nyla drew in air and let it slide out, not as a trick, not as a show—just the truth of a night creature ready to carry the dawn under her coat. She pulled the hood up, gave Kian a look that said bring your clever hands and your boring rules and don't make me use your name, then pushed into the hallway.

They walked together, the two of them in step without trying. The gold not-records watched with their secret grooves. The reel-to-reel winked like it had heard better stories and liked this one anyway. At the back door, Nyla paused with her palm over the plate.

"You don't join Houses," she said, not asking, simply testing the shape of future sentences.

"I build for whoever keeps buildings honest," Kian said. "If you want me to call that joining, I won't argue. I won't kneel."

"No one asked you to kneel," Nyla said. "We prefer a good partner to a bad follower."

He considered that. "Then I'll be a good partner and a worse follower."

"That suits me," she said, and opened the door.

Dawn had begun hazing the edges of things—trash trucks far off, a jogger cutting a line down the block, gulls drawing questions on the light. The label's turquoise sign bled around the corner, softer now, like a secret letting itself be almost seen. The air carried salt and a whisper of iron. The city's appetite rolled under it all.

Nyla slid into her car. Kian stepped back into shadow, already turning toward the work inside. He would dissect lies in cable and seam; she would charm a radio audience into making better mornings. Two parts of the same agenda: keep the pulse honest, keep the hunger pointed the right direction.

Her phone buzzed once. Ardelia: Be ready.

Nyla smiled at the economy. She didn't need prose. She needed clean lines and rooms that didn't lie and a voice in her left ear that could stop her if she forgot herself. The engine woke. The alley gave her to the street.

She drove toward the station, toward a brief performance for people who brewed tea instead of drinking it, toward a city already making plans for the next night she'd take in her hands. She licked a trace of copper from her lip and felt the low steady burn of the House's blend do its work—no fog, no frenzy, all blade.

The sun was coming. Silence would make its moves. The House would answer with song. And Nyla Voss—magnet and lure, saint and predator—rolled into the pale morning with a new engineer on the ledger and a clean line in her throat, ready to turn the entire day until it said yes.

# III

Miami's daylight had decided to pretend it was a soft filter. Palms winked at the breeze. Traffic made promises it couldn't keep. By the time Nyla slid back into Arista House Records for her first official session with Kian, the city felt almost polite about its chaos.

Studio B wore a different mood than A—less cathedral, more workshop. Cozier, with racks tucked along the walls like well-behaved wolves and a plinth table cleared for experiments that would later be explained away as "product development." A low couch waited where artists usually sprawled; today it held a slim flight case and an open velvet tray of House flasks beading in the cool.

Kian was already in the room, sleeves rolled, hair pushed back, two fingers resting lightly on the edge of the console like a stethoscope. He didn't look up right away. He was listening with his hands.

"Checking my pulse?" Nyla said, dropping her bag and setting her sunglasses on the case like she owned the furniture by arrival alone.

"Checking the room," he said, still half-attentive to the wood. "Yours comes through either way."

"Flattery on the first line." She grinned. "You'll spoil me."

"I don't flatter," he said, finally turning. "It wastes time."

"'Hi, good morning, you look fantastic' and other lies," she deadpanned, stepping into the light so it could vote for her.

Kian took her in like he measured furniture—height, balance, center of gravity. Not cold, just efficient. "You look capable," he said. "That covers it."

"Capable." She laughed. "The sexiest adjective."

"If that word isn't in your fan mail, they're writing you wrong."

"Please don't read my fan mail."

"Not interested," he said. "I'm here for the edge where talent tips into trouble."

"That's adorable," she said lightly, moving toward the rack where his case sat open. Inside: coils, micro-drivers, wafer-thin discs arranged with a watchmaker's neatness. "Is this my jewelry that doesn't admit it's jewelry?"

"Beta versions," he said, stepping closer. "One pendant, one cable clip, one under-desk strip. The strip is ugly, which means it'll probably work best. The pendant is prettier, which means you'll wear it."

"Accuse me of vanity again and see what happens."

"Not an accusation," he said. "A design requirement."

Nyla lifted the pendant. Matte black drop, no logo, no shine, suspended on a fine chain. Up close, inside the drop, a faint pattern shifted when she tilted it—coils stacked like a spiral staircase. "How much can this catch?"

"It listens before you do and throws out anything shaped like a loop trying to turn in on itself." He pointed to the back. "Tap here to mute outright. Tap twice to let more through. Don't worry about battery; it sips."

She placed the chain against her throat and clipped it on. Cool, precise weight. "How do I look."

"Capable," he said again, deadpan.

"Stop. I might swoon."

"If you pass out, Marisol will murder me before you hit the floor," he said. "So no."

"I like that you think she can take you," Nyla said, amused. "Let's start."

They built the session simple: headphones routed, booth door propped open to keep the air less formal, flasks within reach on the console. Nyla didn't step into the isolation cube this time. She wanted him up close, wanted to feel the room react with both of them in it.

"Parameters," Kian said, setting a notebook on the console and uncapping a pen that looked like it made lists behave. "I'll sweep sub and low-mid with your baseline tone, then push on purpose. Tell me before your body tells you."

"Bold of you to assume I don't let my body speak first," she said, settling a hand on the console's padded edge. "But fine."

"Also," he added, "I'm not here to fix you. I'm here to build guardrails you'll ignore until you need them."

"That's the first sensible thing you've said."

"It won't be the last."

She rolled her shoulders, shook out the night she still carried, and invited breath into the room. The first tone slid out of her without drama—clean, centered, the column she could stack a city on. The pendant warmed at her collarbone, a gentle yes. The meters rose like attentive faces.

Kian stood just to her right, not touching, close enough that she could see the idea click behind his eyes when the tone widened and the floorboards answered. He didn't sway. He didn't fall into it. He rested his left palm against the rack wood and nodded once.

"You feel that?" she asked, curious.

"In my hand," he said. "Not my ear."

"That's a new sentence."

"It's old for me," he said. "Carpenter father. Engines. Buildings that talk when they're about to stop behaving. Sound moves through material. I like material more than air."

"You'd hate a choir loft," she said, teasing.

"I'd brace it," he said, and she almost smiled.

He pushed a frequency with a light twist. The pendant cooled slightly. The room tucked a stray edge back where it belonged. Clean.

"Again," he said.

She stacked another tone, this time letting joy sit on top—a bright, easy curve. The pendant stayed warm. Kian's hand shifted to the console's side panel. He closed his eyes for a beat, not romantic, diagnostic.

"Midrange wants to bloom," he said. "You shut it down out of habit. I don't want you shutting down anything you need later."

"I like my blooms on purpose," she said.

"Agreed," he said. "So we make the room behave in advance."

She tilted her head. "You really don't hear it?"

"I hear what I need. I feel the rest," he said. "You could pull a wall down with a look. I'd know it through the screws before the sound would warn me."

"That should not be hot," she said under her breath, then louder, "Let's put a glide on it."

She slid into a line that wasn't a note anyone could name but felt like a sunrise poured into a glass. Kian tapped the under-desk strip he'd mounted earlier. The air shifted—edges softer without going dull. The pendant purred against skin. Good. Strong.

He raised two fingers. "Now tempt me."

She blinked. "Excuse me?"

"Whatever you call it when you decide a room should love you. Do that." He set his palm on the rack again. "Let's see what the pendant lets through."

Nyla laughed. "You want the siren without the ocean? Cute."

"I want to know if your trick bounces off me," he said. "And if it does, what the room does with the ricochet."

"You're a scientist. How depressing."

"I'm an engineer," he corrected mildly. "We build for outcomes. Your outcome is messy joy with no hangover. That requires data."

"Fine," she said, amused and absolutely interested. She pulled the charm up from her chest and let it rest against her throat like a talisman, then turned and gave him what most people paid cover to receive: the slow tilt of a head that says I see you, the half-smile that promises I might keep seeing you, the easy velvet in her voice that pours yes into a person's ribs before they can mount a defense.

"Hey," she said. "Pay attention."

He did. He didn't sway toward her.

Nothing else in the room lurched either—no glass chimed, no cable lifted. The pendant warmed, then cooled, like it had processed something and filed it under Not For Us.

Kian lifted his hand from the wood. "Do it again."

She pushed a little more—still tasteful, still controlled, the kind she used to encourage a crowd to drink water, to step back from an edge, to fall in love with their own night.

Kian blinked. Once. "I feel it in the panel, not in my head," he said, almost curious, not bothered. "Like silk pulled over wood."

"That metaphoric thinking will get you in trouble," Nyla said, masking the flicker of surprise with a joke. Her pull didn't miss often. It hadn't missed at all since she'd learned discipline. "Third time."

"You're escalating."

"Data," she said sweetly, and let a sharper sweetness coat the next words. "You want me to say please?"

He smiled, brief. "I like it when you do, but it's not required."

"Please," she said, letting the syllable slide.

Kian leaned closer to the side panel, not to her. "It answers in the wall," he said. "Not in me. Your voice lands like the room is the one falling for you and I'm the chaperone."

"That is the most irritating thing anyone has said to me this month," she said, even as something like relief braided with thrill in her chest. "Ardelia will love you."

"I'm not here to be loved," he said. "I'm here to make sure the building doesn't give you false promises."

"You realize my entire job is selling promises," she said.

"Promises you keep," he said.

She couldn't argue that. She didn't want to.

They ran practical drills. He jogged sub by single-decibel kisses and watched how the pendant behaved. She tilted tone and feeling to see which emotions the circuit let through with no interference. Joy, yes. Relief, yes. Desire, yes—but tempered, somehow, not diluted, just given boundaries. Panic? The pendant cooled and pushed back. Good. Grief? It opened like a door, then sorted grief into manageable portions, and Nyla didn't realize she'd closed her eyes until Kian said, not unkindly, "Stay with me."

"I'm here," she said, and she was.

On the third series, he set both hands on the console frame for a longer length of time, eyes half-closed, attention sunk deep into the material.

"Does it hurt?" she asked.

"No," he said. "It's clearer than people."

"That's a read."

"It wasn't meant to be," he said. "Buildings tell the truth even when they creak."

"People tell prettier stories," she said.

"That's why we put them in rooms that won't lie," he said, and she conceded the point with a tilt of her head.

He moved around the console, palms down, fingers spread, working the perimeter like one of those old-school dowsers searching for wells. Up close, she noted the small things: a scar across his knuckle like a pencil line, the steadiness that never tipped into stiffness, the way his breath stayed even while he listened.

"Try your pull again," he said without looking up. "But swing it wide. Aim at the space, not me."

"You sure?"

"Yes."

She widened the net. Not heavy-handed, not predatory; she wasn't here to wreck a lab. She gave the room affection the way you give a skittish dog a palm to smell. The pendant warmed, then settled. Kian's jaw loosened by a fraction—absorbing the shift, not succumbing to it.

"I feel it," he said, hands still over wood. "Like a low tide going out, leaving the floor clean."

"That image is going to live rent-free," she said. "Congrats."

"Does my lack of response annoy you?" he asked, glancing up.

"It unsettles me," she said honestly. "I don't break toys, and I'm not a toy. I use the power because it helps people do what they came to do. They want to move. They want to breathe. Sometimes they want to fall in love with their own mirror. I'm a shortcut."

"Shortcut implies cheating," he said. "What you do is infrastructure."

"You're dangerously close to flattering me."

"Observation," he said.

She tried the pull one more time, a private version she usually saved for coaxing an anxious chandelier of a room back to steadiness. Kian braced lightly on the left side of the desk, eyes closing for a heart-count. When he opened them, he had an answer.

"It hits me if I put skin on wood," he said. "If I lift off, it rolls past. So either my nerves translate sound into pressure or you're better on furniture than on men."

"That's a t-shirt," she said, delighted. "I'm better on furniture."

"Put it on merch," he said, straight-faced.

"Do you ever smile like a full person," she said. "Or do you ration those like flasks."

"Occasional," he said. "When people surprise me."

"Have I not done that already?"

"You have," he said. "But I'm working."

She tossed him a look and reached for a flask. "I'm taking a sip."

"Citrus blend?" he asked.

"Ardelia's favorite," she said. "Keeps me pointed in the right direction." The draw steadied everything that had started to flutter on the edges. He watched, present without gawking, which she appreciated more than she let on.

"Again," he said after a beat, and they were running a different sequence—call-and-response tests, micro-breaks by design, establishing a vocabulary neither of them had to write down.

When the first hour snapped past, he walked to the plinth table and slid a square case toward her. "Headphone clip," he said. "Same circuit as the pendant. If you can't wear jewelry, this rides the cable and pretends it's part of your look."

"Nothing pretends with my look," she said, clipping it near the Y-split. The clip warmed instantly, a friendly little battery of a thing. "How do I keep from accidentally muting it mid-set?"

"You won't," he said. "The tap surface needs a deliberate press. Also, I'm going to build you muscle memory. Tap before every drop. You'll resent me until it saves you."

She gave him a mock salute. "You've met me for five minutes and you think you're training me. Brave."

"I think you're already disciplined," he said. "I'm giving your discipline new tools."

She didn't say thank you. She didn't need to. He heard it anyway in the way she held the clip like it wasn't just hardware.

They shifted to music—the fun kind, not lab tones. Nyla rolled in a stripped-down loop from a set she'd retired last summer, a sunny keyboard climb under a tight kick. Kian's palm flattened on the desk again. He watched the way the loop changed shape when she smiled into it. Some people said "vibe" and let that excuse their lack of craft. With Nyla, craft made the vibe possible. The room brightened.

"You feel that?" she asked.

"Through the frame," he said. "It's like your smile adds a small lift to the wood. The screws like you."

"The screws like me," she repeated, laughing. "Put it on a cake."

"That's a terrible cake," he said. "But yes."

She cut the loop to silence. The pendant cooled with it. For a breath, the room held a clean quiet—the kind after a kiss that everyone pretends wasn't a kiss.

"Honest opinion," she said. "You were at the club. You saw me dodge the snag. If I hadn't, how bad would it have been?"

"Not catastrophic," he said. "You're too good. But the crowd would've left with a tightness they couldn't name. They'd sleep, wake up irritated, think it was their boss or their roommate or the wrong eggs. It wouldn't be the eggs."

"So a petty day for half the city," she said. "We don't do petty."

"No," he said. "We do clean. Which is why we're here."

Fun found them more easily after that. He made two deadpan jokes about her sequins having better posture than some sound techs he'd met; she called him "structural integrity in linen" and watched his mouth twitch like it couldn't help itself. He explained the difference between a room that sang along and a room that tried to solo. She explained how to hold a group at the exact temperature where strangers become allies. Neither of them admitted out loud that the other's language turned into pictures they didn't hate.

She tried the pull one last time, out of pure curiosity, smaller than before, shaped like an invitation instead of a command. He looked up, met her eye, and—this time—she watched the smallest echo touch him. Not desire. Not awe. Something simpler and more promising: attention without guard.

"There it is," she said, satisfied.

"I let you have that," he said.

"Sure you did," she answered, and both of them knew he'd told the truth and she'd found her opening anyway.

Marisol appeared in the doorway, leaning on the frame like a pin-up for patience. "How's my favorite science couple?"

"We're not a couple," Kian said at the exact second Nyla said, "Terrible and thriving."

"Perfect," Marisol said, unfazed. She set a new tray in the console's shadow—fresh flasks with a tiny X scored into the glass, a House shorthand for extra-clean blend. "Radio car is downstairs at two-thirty. Ardelia says tell the host to keep his hands on the desk. His left, specifically."

"Of course it's his left," Nyla muttered.

"Anything we need to rearrange before she goes?" Marisol asked Kian.

"Pedal chain is rerouted," he said. "Left seam is braced temporarily. The under-desk strip is ugly but effective."

"My condolences," Marisol said solemnly. "Beauty later. Function now."

"Exactly," he said.

She winked at Nyla. "Don't break the engineer."

"I haven't even tried," Nyla said.

"Don't," Kian said dryly, and Marisol's laughter floated down the hall as she left.

When they were alone again, the air felt easier. First sessions usually went one of two ways: ego chess or instant choir. This had become a third thing—sparring with a scoreboard neither of them would admit to keeping.

Nyla lifted the pendant chain, considered it, and let it fall. "You really don't respond to my voice."

"I respond to your skill," he said. "Your voice rides the room; the room sends the message; my hands get it. Ears are optional."

"That will save your life and make mine complicated," she said, not unhappy.

"I'll take the first half," he said. "You can have the second."

She checked the time. Two-twenty. "Walk me down?"

"I'm not your security."

"You're my engineer," she said. "You care about doorways."

"True," he said, grabbing his case. "Also," he added, almost as an afterthought, "you call me Redd on paper. It avoids confusion."

"Kian Redd," she said, tasting the rhythm of it in her mouth—careful: not that word—tasting the cadence. "All right, Redd. Keep up."

They moved through the corridor of fake records and real power. Staff pretended not to watch them pass. A junior tech pressed himself to the wall like he was making space for royalty, which neither of them corrected because it would have been rude to deny the kid his story later.

At the back door, Kian paused and pressed a hand to the frame again. "Clear," he said. "But your radio host is going to flirt."

"He flirts with anything that has breath and a rating," Nyla said. "He can flirt with the door."

"If he touches you, I'll be disappointed."

"He won't," she said, almost bored. "I'm fun, not free."

Kian addressed the door, because apparently that's who he talked to when he didn't want to say something to a person. "You heard her."

She laughed, genuinely. "You're ridiculous."

"Capable," he corrected, deadpan. "Go make the morning forget it's morning."

"Meet me here at four," she said. "Bring the clip in silver. And something for the booth that doesn't look like a submarine."

"I'll bring two somethings and a backup," he said.

She pulled the hood up, let the pendant rest against her throat, and stepped into the bright day. The radio car idled by the curb—music station logo plastered on the door, driver checking her phone like she was praying for cancellations. Nyla turned once, caught Kian watching not her but the hinge as it closed, and found that both maddening and weirdly comforting.

"Redd," she called.

He looked up.

“Try smiling at least once before lunch,” she said. “It’ll confuse your enemies.”

His mouth curved one degree. “That would be you.”

“Not yet,” she said, and slid into the car.

The door shut. The pendant warmed. The city moved. And somewhere between a booth with good bones and a radio station with bad coffee, the next piece of the fun began—because she’d finally found someone who felt her music with his hands and refused to be charmed by anything but the work. That wasn’t a problem. That was a dare.

# IV

Dusk laid itself over Brickell like a silk scarf—peach at the edges, violet toward the center, city lights testing their brightness against a sky that hadn't made up its mind yet. The private rooftop party had language for itself: exclusive, invite-only, intentionally intimate. Translation: enough people to start a religion if someone got the pitch right.

Nyla stepped from the elevator into golden hour that made everyone look like a better version of themselves. Glass balustrades, low white couches, planters fat with tropical leaves. A bar wrapped in linen at the far end offered "bespoke spritzes" to mortals and, for House usage only, a cooler tucked beneath with neatly labeled flasks. Music travel case in one hand, hoodie in the other, she looked like the kind of DJ who didn't break a sweat because she refused to wear it.

"Ms. Voss." The host—Rafael with the too-white smile and the kind of watch that could sponsor a small opera—met her at the crest of the stairs. He wasn't House, but he rented House-adjacent glamour and paid on time. "The sunset is yours."

"That's a dangerous gift," Nyla said lightly, even as she glanced around. The skyline cut a jagged halo of windows; the bay in the distance threw back a coin of light. The crowd already leaned toward the booth. The booth loved them for it.

Kian was there before she was, sleeves rolled, slate again because apparently he lived there. He was on one knee beside the under-desk strip, as if praying to a god made of cables. When he saw her, he didn't stand immediately. He splayed his fingers against the booth's wood and slid his palm along it, eyes narrowing in thought. Listening.

"Good bones?" Nyla asked, setting her case on the stand.

"Decent," he said, rising. "Railing glass is too lively. Floor panels are tight. Power is clean." He tapped the edge. "Open air does half the work. It's forgiving."

"I'm not," she said, smiling because she wanted the room to catch it. "We'll be merciful anyway."

Rafael made promises about "the best crowd in the city" and "no cops by nine" and then melted into his guests. Kian double-checked her pendant clip, brushed his thumb over the under-desk strip, and set a small, nondescript square the size of a coaster beneath the booth's lip.

"What's that one do?" Nyla asked.

"Listens," he said. "Tells me when the room tries to sing for you without permission."

"Jealous."

"Protective," he said, which, from him, almost counted as charm.

She laid hands on the board. Dusk breathed across her arms. Miami sent up its evening perfume—ocean salt, hot stone, lipstick, gin, a faint ripple of iron from her case. She drew breath, reached into that air like a sculptor feeling for the lines under stone, and then—music.

She didn't start big. She tucked a soft synth line just beneath the chatter so people would hear it only when they'd been invited. A hi-hat kissed the horizon. Bass didn't arrive yet; she let the city's own heartbeat do that work.

Heads turned like flowers angling toward sun.

Nyla spun jam and ease as if they were physical materials—the tones sticky-sweet, just enough grip on the edges to give the body permission. She threaded her voice through the first transition, not words, just a sound that felt like a breeze on the back of someone's neck telling them to exhale. People did, without checking who ordered it.

Kian watched the meters and didn't blink much. He had one palm down on the booth, as if anyone else would try to run with her. She let herself be pleased that he kept the board steady with the same focus he'd use to hold a bridge.

She fed—not with teeth. House work demanded elegance. The joy that rose from the floor reached her throat like a pleasant fizz. She took a measured sip, let it settle. Smile for the banker's wife whose shoulders had been up around her ears since March; little nod for the girl who hadn't stopped dancing since the elevator; the briefest glance for the man in the corner who'd decided not to leave his marriage tonight after all.

"Too easy?" Kian asked, voice low, eyes on his puzzle.

"Earned," she said, and tucked more percussion under the skyline.

The pendant warmed against her throat—affirmation. The new clip listened and threw back the right trash before she had to. The room adjusted to her hand like a good partner. Open air meant the sound could lift without getting trapped. She laced a vocal run through the mix and felt a seam in the glass balustrade flutter. Kian's fingers shifted; the flutter smoothed. They were good. They could be great.

Rafael drifted past, clapping a little too loud, and said something about after-party yachts. Nyla waved him away with a smile that tasted like yes but meant I'm working.

The sun flirted with the horizon and decided to lose. The light slipped bluer; the city lit itself. A woman near the bar put her hand to her throat and laughed quietly in a way that said: I caught the exact moment the night turned on.

Nyla eased the bass in—not a slam, a hello. The floor answered with a taut pleasure that slid across her palms. She fed again, a careful draw, letting the crowd keep more than she took. Clean. Clean. She tasted a flash of fear from someone near the planter—first time above the twelfth floor—and wrapped it in a chord that settled the vestibular argument their inner ear was having. Fear softened. She took a sip of that, a reward from the universe for good behavior.

A dancer in steel flats sketched shapes in the last of the light. Nyla timed a clap to her turn, and the crowd acknowledged a choreography none of them had rehearsed. This was what she loved—when people's bodies remembered they'd always had music in them and didn't need instructions to find it.

She went wider, letting her siren voice sweep the edges of the deck. Heads tilted. Temples cooled. Mouths softened. Not desire yet. Reception.

Kian raised his eyes from the board to the crowd, scanning, then back to the rail glass. His right hand flexed once; nerves testing field. "So far so good," he said.

"So far so beautiful," she corrected.

The House would have called this dinner. Not a feast; that would be later, under lights. This was the part where you decide which dishes belong on your table and which you'll send to the pass for someone else to taste. Nyla's palate was simple: joy, relief, courage, permission. She took a ribbon of each and let the rest spin back to the dancers.

Sunset finally fell off the edge. Blue deepened. The first star pretended it wasn't a plane.

Nyla winked at the city and gave them a bass run that sat just right in the hips, then added a glittering run of keys. Feeds slid into place. The pendant warmed; the clip stayed content. She felt the good electricity gather in her sternum and spread—the kind that didn't steal, the kind that paid. The crowd felt it too; conversation turned to breath turned to laughter turned to movement.

Then something on the breeze changed its mind.

It wasn't a wind shift—not that simple. It felt like an echo from a song she hadn't played yet. The pendant cooled without warning. The crowd's laughter sharpened by a degree you'd miss if you weren't trained to hear it. Her tongue tasted a metallic edge not from the flasks.

"Kian," she said, too low for anyone else, "do you—"

"Left pane," he said, already moving his hand to the under-desk strip. "The glass started singing."

"I didn't ask it to."

"It wants to," he said, which was not reassuring.

She reduced the high end by a hair. The pendant warmed again. Relief. The deck settled. Good. She sent a low sweep through the floor—the House's way of telling a room to behave. The panels purred, if floors purred. Guests laughed at the pleasant shiver under their shoes and laughed again because you don't get floors like this at home.

Nyla kissed the mic. "If the view makes you forget your name, you can borrow mine," she said, letting velvet ride the joke. Gentle ripple. It returned to her like sparkling water. She took a sip.

Then the power spiked.

Not the building's—her own.

It started as a small, slippery thrill. She was used to them. Night work had taught her what happened when she leaned too hard into the yes and the yes leaned back. But this felt… synthetic. The echo came not from the crowd but from the perimeter. Not the floorboard, the glass. A loop closed somewhere she hadn't drawn.

The pendant stuttered hot-cold-hot. The clip blipped warning patterns against her collarbone. The air went thinner by one notch. Her throat cut a cleaner line than she'd ordered.

The bodies on the deck didn't know why they suddenly needed to touch someone. A laugh veered into a near-shout. A man put his hand on a stranger's shoulder and neither of them moved it. Someone near the planters took a half step out of their own body and then backed back in, startled.

"Kian," Nyla said, keeping her smile fixed as she adjusted nothing at all in a way that said I'm adjusting everything. "Mirrors?"

"None. It's the glass." His eyes cut to the far end where the railing curved and caught the bay like a bowl. "It's throwing your voice back with an extra coat of sugar."

"I didn't order sugar."

"Someone did."

House of Silence loved sugar that tasted like control.

"Fix it," she said, polite teeth.

"Working," he said, fingers moving over the strip. "Can't change the bay. Can tell the board to ignore it."

The pendant cooled. The city pressed against her skin. The feeling many people chased in a room like this — God, I could live here forever — tilted into something that had less God and more need. If she pulled now, she'd get a lot. Too much. The wrong balance. She could choke herself with it.

"Hold," she told herself. To the crowd: "Breathe."

They did because her voice told their lungs what to do and human biology is honest when music gets involved.

Someone near the bar started crying, friendly-tears, the kind that say this is the best night of my life; someone else bared their throat to the wind and thought they were a myth. Two men laughed too loud; a woman touched the pulse at her neck with a wonder that wasn't about jewelry. The tilt became sharper.

"Stop," Kian said, right in her ear, quiet and firm enough to make her hand freeze over the fader.

"You don't tell me — "

"Stop," he repeated, not louder. "The glass is lying to your pendant. It's telling it everything is a welcome mat. It's not."

She pulled the high end down hard enough to deny herself candy. The crowd booed without knowing why. She smiled at them and gave them a clap pattern that changed their mood to playful. It helped, but the undercurrent kept tugging in the wrong direction. Her throat wanted more and her body wanted more and the deck kept offering.

She didn't cut because she didn't cut. She managed because she was a professional. She could throttle resonance without bruising. She had a thousand tricks before breaking glass.

And then a pocket near the corner tipped past thrill into frenzy. How do you know? A hand clenched too long on a stranger's wrist. A laugh that didn't end. A door in someone's pupils opening the wrong way.

Kian moved.

He didn't reach for her board. He stepped around her, planted a hand on the under-desk strip, and hit the silent square he'd tucked beneath the lip.

The sound went out like a candle.

Not silence—rooftop parties don't know silence. Traffic below, building ventilation, the human sounds of surprise. But music, gone. Her line cut clean.

The pendant cooled to neutral. The clip went inert. The wrong tilt dropped, leaving a sharp-edged quiet where joy had been. People blinked, as if waking from a dream they liked. Most laughed like they'd been caught singing. Two leaned on the railing, breathing hard. One sat down out of good sense and let the sky steady them.

Nyla's mouth stayed a smile because the crowd needed it. Her eyes found Kian and turned into something else.

"What did you do," she said, with the kind of calm that meant the question was a placeholder for three that had knives.

"Cut the feed." He kept his body between her and the guests, shield-like. "If you'd pulled in that moment, they would've given you everything because you asked. Then hated you tomorrow because their bodies remembered they didn't mean to."

"I don't take what isn't offered."

"The glass offered in their voice. That's the lie."

She stared at him, throat flickering between gratitude and offended skill. "You don't cut my set."

"I cut a loop." He met her eyes. Unfazed. Factual. "You think I like doing that on a roof full of investors?"

"Sabotage," she said, because the word came faster than the truth.

"Rescue," he said, and didn't move.

Rafael arrived, nervous-laughing. "Breaker popped? We love a pause! Everyone take in the—"

"Three minutes," Kian told him, already flipping the manual bypass on the strip. "We're resetting so your chandelier guests don't start climbing things."

Rafael blinked at that and had enough sense to step aside.

Nyla wasn't rattled often. Not by promoters or techs or district managers pretending to be kings. She was rattled now, and the worst part was that the rattling wasn't anger—it was a piece of hunger looking at Kian and finding nothing to hold.

She leaned in, close enough for the pendant to brush his shirt. "My power doesn't work on you, does it."

"It works on spaces," he said steadily. "It works on people who want it. I feel your music in my hands. My head stays mine."

"You could have said that before you cut my song."

"I wanted to know if the room would try to use me to get to you," he said. "It didn't. That matters."

She hated that she respected the answer. She hated that her body expected the old trick to soften his eyes and the old trick hopscotched to the booth instead, leaving him unbent. She hated, a little, that it was thrilling.

"Don't cut me in public again," she said, because pride needed to be fed even when it was wrong.

"Then don't let a lie sing with you," he said, unfazed. "I'll build you a filter that treats glass like a wall, not a choir. Until then, I kill sugar when sugar tries to drown you."

"Stop calling it sugar," she said, almost laughing despite herself. "You make it sound cheap."

"It is cheap," he said. "Your work isn't."

He toggled the strip. The undercurrent in the air smoothed. The pendant warmed to a polite yes. He looked at her. "Two choices. We pivot to an acoustic set with a live percussionist—your man in steel flats can lead—or we keep it electronic and low, with the clip doing more lifting. Either way, you feed on joy they meant to give you."

"You really think a live set on a Brickell roof is safe?"

"I think anything you control is safer than something controlling you."

She let out a breath she hadn't admitted she was holding. "Live," she said. "And a little electronics for glitter."

He flagged the dancer with a hand signal that said come play, and the dancer came, delighted, grabbing a hand drum from a lean musician who had been pretending to be a guest. Nyla rolled a loop that left space for real hands to matter. The deck recalibrated.

The next half hour tasted clean again. She kept the pull light; Kian kept his palm on the wood. The crowd reset into themselves—laughs back to human sized, touches looking like choices instead of orders. Rafael pretended he'd planned this all along and stopped pretending the third time a guest hugged him for no reason.

When the sun finally finished leaving and the city took over entirely, Nyla let the music settle into a lower lane and gave them an ending that felt like a promise kept. Applause rose, honest sound without sugar.

After, while Rafael made speeches about donations and sunsets and how this wasn't the best party in Miami but the most "intentional," Nyla stepped just out of hearing with Kian near the stairwell.

"Sabotage was rude," she said.

"I'll accept rude," he said. "I won't accept frenzy."

"You cut my power."

"I cut the lie that was about to use your power," he said. "There's a difference, and I need you to know I know it."

She turned the pendant in her fingers, thinking about how his silence—whatever shield lived in him that made her pull slide off and land in the furniture—poked at her hunger and made it misbehave. Not more. Not bigger. Different. The part of her that could devour a crowd by accident found itself paused in front of a man who felt music with his palms and would rather brace a building than bow to a song.

"I accused you of something you didn't do," she said, the words a little harder than a confession because she liked losing even less than she liked being saved.

"You accused me to my face," he said. "That I can work with."

"You saved my crowd."

"I saved your name," he said, simple as stating the time.

A gust tugged at them. Below, the city made the sounds cities make when you step away from them—car horns further than they feel from the ground, laughter lifted by wind, a siren in the distance heading somewhere that would not be this roof.

Nyla looked at him, the square jaw unromantic in the best way, the hands that spoke a language she didn't. "You're immune."

"I'm not a wall," he said. "I just choose which doors to open."

"That's worse," she said, oddly pleased. "It's personal."

"Good," he said. "Keep it that way."

She returned to the deck and gave the room a closing smile that didn't try to own anyone. Kian set his palm on the booth again, included it in the goodbye. The balustrade glass, chastened or bored, stayed a pane and not a choir.

As the first guests drifted toward the elevator, Rafael sidled up, relief operating him like a puppet. "Brilliant," he said. "Unexpected. So real. We're doing a series."

"Pay the invoice on time," Nyla said, and Rafael nodded with the eagerness of a man who'd just been spared a headline.

Back at the booth, Kian passed her one of the fresh flasks from the cooler. Not citrus—something deeper, grounded, warmed by spice. She took a measured draw. It steadied the wrong shimmer in her nerves that the glass had tried to teach her.

"Tomorrow," he said, "we build you a filter that treats bay reflections like stubborn cousins. And we find out who taught your host's contractor to be cute with railings."

"You think it was taught."

"The angle was polished," he said. "It felt intentional."

"Silence?"

"Could be," he said. "Could be an idiot with a shiny catalog. Either way, we fix our side."

She set the flask down, the pendant warm on her throat. "Next time you cut me, give me a signal first."

"I said stop twice."

"I was working."

"Exactly," he said.

She almost laughed. "You're going to be exhausting."

"I'm going to be useful," he said, and for the first time since the music died, she let that comfort her.

Morning arrived in Miami without apology.

Heat unrolled itself over the city, pulling yesterday's glitter into a sticky haze. Palms leaned in like gossiping neighbors, their fronds whispering about whatever happened on the rooftop last night.

By ten a.m., the rumor already had a name: *the hum.*

Nyla woke to it—not the sound itself, but the shape of it. The faint, phantom vibration under her ribs that shouldn't have been there. Her phone blinked alive on the nightstand, buried under a tangle of headphone cables. Five missed calls, three messages from Marisol, one from a number she didn't recognize, and a single push alert from *SpinWire Miami*:

**DJ SIVAN FOUND DEAD IN STUDIO**

Her stomach dropped, not from guilt, but from recognition.

She knew that name.

Sivan had opened for her two weeks ago at Midnight Tempo. Arrogant, loud, good in the way amateurs often are—fast hands, big talk, no discipline. He'd laughed about "catching up to the House" one day. He hadn't realized he was speaking prophecy.

Nyla scrolled through the article, watching the screen light her palm.

"...local DJ Sivan Cruz was discovered unresponsive in his South Beach studio early this morning. Investigators have not released a cause of death, but witnesses reported hearing loud feedback and a sustained hum through the night. Police confirmed the track was still looping when they entered..."

She read that line twice.

House rumor spread faster than the internet. By the time she reached the safehouse, she'd passed two vampires leaning against a mural arguing about whether Sivan had bitten his own tongue off mid-track. Others claimed his system had shorted while he was feeding—fried by resonance. The details changed with every retelling, but the accusation under it didn't.

They thought it was her.

Inside Arista, the front sign glowed too bright for morning. Interns kept their heads down, and the elevator ride to the third floor felt longer than it ever had. She could taste the tension through the metal—electric, metallic, half-truth flavored.

Marisol met her at the door to Studio A, eyes sharp over a cup of something crimson that wasn't coffee. "You heard."

"I read."

"Then you know the Council's already sniffing."

Nyla blew out a slow breath. "I was hoping you'd say rumor control."

Marisol's laugh was humorless. "Rumor control died with him. Ardelia's on the line with them now. They're calling it a *resonance casualty.*"

"That's not a real category."

"It is now."

The door to Ardelia's office was closed, the glass frosted and humming faintly—privacy wards. Nyla felt them vibrate against her skin when she pushed inside.

Ardelia stood at the center of the room, phone at her ear, back to the skyline. The morning sun turned the silk of her robe into molten amber.

"No," she was saying, perfectly calm. "My artists feed clean. Midnight Tempo operates under code. We don't mix mortal sets with House sessions. I will cooperate, of course."

A pause.

Her eyes slid toward Nyla. "Yes," she said, quiet now. "She's here."

She ended the call without farewell, which meant it wasn't really over.

"They think it was me," Nyla said before Ardelia could start.

"They think it was us," Ardelia corrected. "Midnight Tempo sits under my protection. The Council doesn't separate the artist from the House when the body count starts."

Nyla crossed her arms. "You believe them?"

"I believe you were feeding last night," Ardelia said, moving toward the console where a small transmitter pulsed with silent information. "I believe Sivan's studio was less than two miles from your rooftop, and the frequencies from both events crossed in the bay."

Nyla frowned. "That's impossible. The glass was the problem, not the water."

Ardelia gave her a look that said *you know better.* "Everything in this city conducts. You play through its veins. You think the tide doesn't listen?"

For a moment, the room felt like it inhaled.

Nyla looked away. "He was an idiot, but he didn't deserve that."

Ardelia's tone softened by a degree. "No one deserves resonance death. The Council wants to call it a relapse. A warning sign."

"You told them it wasn't."

"I told them it couldn't be proven," Ardelia said. "Which is not the same thing."

Nyla's jaw clenched. "They're going to shut us down."

"They're going to investigate first," Ardelia said. "And yes, they'll send auditors to the club, to your sets, maybe even your flat. Until then, you will be quiet. No public appearances. No interviews. You'll keep your music inside these walls."

"And if I don't?"

Ardelia's voice went soft, dangerous. "Then you'll make their case for them."

The silence between them filled with all the things they didn't say—the rooftop, the glass, the wrongness that had crawled under her pendant when the bay sang back.

Finally, Ardelia moved to the sideboard and poured a vial into a shallow glass. "Drink. You're shaking."

Nyla hadn't realized she was. She took the glass and swallowed. It tasted like winter air and steadiness. Her hunger receded enough to think straight.

Ardelia watched her over the rim of her own drink. "Kian's been summoned, too. The Council wants his testimony about the rooftop incident."

Nyla's head snapped up. "He'll tell them what happened."

"He'll tell the truth," Ardelia said. "Which is rarely the same thing."

Nyla set the glass down hard enough for the table to click. "I'm not hiding while they turn my name into an excuse. Sivan's death wasn't an accident. Someone built that loop to kill him."

Ardelia didn't deny it. "And what do you think you'll find if you go digging?"

"The person who's trying to make me look like a weapon," Nyla said.

"The Council will call it defiance," Ardelia warned. "They'll say you're chasing blood to hide the taste of your own."

"Then let them talk," Nyla said, voice sharpening into resolve. "I'm not sitting here while they decide my fate over coffee and flasks."

Ardelia sighed. "You are impossible."

"You trained me that way."

That earned her the faintest hint of a smile. "Then you'd better be as good as I made you."

For a moment, Nyla lingered—half out of respect, half to let her pulse align with the quiet thrum that kept the House alive. The morning light spilled across the studio's frosted windows, brushing Ardelia's profile in gold. No recoil, no hiss, no vanishing into shadow. Their kind hadn't done that in a century.

The old rules had burned away with the old world.

When the Council first formalized the Houses—Sound, Silence, Smoke, and Stone—they hadn't just carved society into clans. They had rewritten survival. The ritual was called *The Tempering*: an infusion of engineered blood and resonance that tethered them to the Earth's own circadian rhythm. They no longer burned in the sun; they merely ached in it. As long as they fed cleanly—on emotion, not flesh—the light would tolerate them.

That tolerance came at a cost. The day made them slower, hungrier, stripped of the glamour that came so easily at night. Their beauty dulled around the edges, their senses turned down like a dimmer switch. They called it *Dayfade*—a harmless name for something that felt like walking through the world wrapped in fog. Most of them preferred to sleep through it. Ardelia didn't. Neither did Nyla.

The Maestra once said daylight was the House's penance for evolution—proof that even monsters had learned moderation.

Nyla never fully believed that. To her, the sun wasn't mercy. It was just another kind of stage light.

She tightened her hood, feeling the faint weight of her pendant against her throat—its metal cool, the blood in its core still alive from last night's feeding. As long as it pulsed, she could stand the day. As long as she kept moving, she could pretend the sun didn't make her bones feel too heavy for her skin.

She gave Ardelia one last glance. "I'll find out who did this."

"I know you will," the Maestra said. "But don't mistake endurance for invincibility."

Nyla smiled, thin and sharp. "Wouldn't dream of it."

Then she turned toward the door. The light beyond it shimmered like an open mouth, and she walked straight through.

The studio door shut behind her like a promise.

Kian was in the corridor, leaning against the wall, his expression unreadable. He'd traded the linen for black denim, sleeves rolled, cable ties looped around his wrist like bracelets. The kind of man who looked like he could fix a bridge or break one depending on his mood.

"You heard," she said.

"Half the city has," he said. "Council already pinged me. They want my logs from the rooftop."

"You keep logs?"

"I keep everything."

Nyla started down the hall; he fell into step beside her. "I didn't kill him," she said.

"I know."

"You sound certain."

"I was there when you lost control," he said. "You didn't lose that far."

"Thanks for the compliment."

"Wasn't one."

They passed the gold-record hallway—the ones that weren't records at all—and stepped into the morning glare bleeding through the front lobby windows. Outside, the city looked oblivious. Inside, it felt like a verdict waiting to happen.

Kian stopped at the door. "Lay low. That's Ardelia's line, right?"

"She means it."

"She also knows you won't."

Nyla turned to face him. "You think the hum killed him?"

"I think someone wanted it to look like it did. The track he was working on—" He paused, pulled out his phone, thumbed through a file, and played three seconds of low-quality audio.

A faint throb. Then a pulse underneath it—too human, too hungry.

It made her teeth ache.

She touched her chest unconsciously, where the pendant lay cool against her skin. "That's not a resonance pattern. That's mimicry."

"Exactly." Kian's eyes met hers. "Someone's feeding through recordings now. That's how you scale a murder."

The words sank in like anchors.

Nyla had seen what resonance could do when it fractured—a single scream that melted speakers, a set that accidentally rewired three hearts at once—but this was different. Someone was shaping it, bottling it.

"Who benefits from that?" she murmured.

"Whoever wants the Council to outlaw live sets," Kian said. "Whoever wants the House of Sound silenced."

Nyla's mind flashed to the rival factions, the hushed arguments, the way the House of Silence had crept closer every month. They'd been lobbying to replace live feeding with controlled resonance for years. To take the risk—and the artistry—out of their nature.

She looked at Kian. "Silence is making songs."

He nodded. "And one just killed a man."

The thought made her hunger twist. Not from desire—from something that felt like fear wearing curiosity's mask.

Nyla turned toward the exit. "Then we find out where that track came from."

"And if Ardelia forbids it?"

"She can forbid my performances. Not my instincts."

Kian hesitated for only a breath. Then he followed. "You're going to get us both dragged before the Council."

"Maybe," she said. "But if they're going to accuse me of losing control, I might as well prove I haven't."

Outside, the heat pressed closer, sticky with salt and conspiracy. The city thrummed beneath their feet, still holding the echo of the hum.

Nyla tucked her sunglasses into her hair, straightened, and started toward Sivan's studio across the bay. Behind her, Kian's footsteps matched hers exactly—steady, deliberate, and far too calm for what they were walking into.

Above them, the sky shone like polished glass, and for the first time since the rooftop, Nyla wondered whether it was listening.

# VI

The club looked different in daylight—hungover but defiant.

Sunlight fractured across its mirrored façade, bouncing off the sea, slicing through the glass to paint the walls in thin, trembling lines. Midnight Tempo wasn't built for mornings, but it endured them anyway—like most creatures who lived too long in the dark.

Nyla and Kian stepped inside through the service entrance, both wearing sunglasses that had less to do with style and more with biology. The club's main floor still smelled faintly of last night's perfume and ozone. Speakers dozed in silence. Empty glasses waited like tiny, accusing ghosts.

"You're quiet," Kian said, running his hand along the booth rail.

"I'm thinking," she replied, stepping up beside him. "Don't sound so surprised."

"Didn't say I was."

"Good. Because I'm dangerous when I think."

He made a noise halfway between amusement and concern. "Define dangerous."

"I'll let you know after coffee," she said, then tilted her head toward the far hall. "The archives are in sublevel one. Ardelia keeps the old masters there—stuff that predates digital. Reel-to-reel, sealed vinyl, frequency tests from the first House sessions."

"You think Sivan's death connects to an archive file?"

"I think whoever corrupted his track knew what they were borrowing from."

Before he could answer, a voice echoed down the stairwell—bubbly, melodic, and entirely out of sync with the tension crawling through the air.

"Oh my *god*, you're here early! I thought you vampires slept until the next moonrise!"

The voice came with a blur of motion—a young woman bounding up the stairs two at a time, blonde curls bouncing, red sunglasses perched in her hair like a crown. She wore a T-shirt that read *DON'T ASK MY AGE (I WON'T TELL YOU THE TRUTH)*, cutoff denim shorts, and sneakers dusted with glitter.

"Kian Redd, meet Tavi," Nyla said, without bothering to hide her sigh.

"Tavi," he echoed, blinking once.

"Short for Octavia," she said cheerfully, extending a hand. "Half-vamp, half-human, half-terrific."

"That's three halves," Kian said.

She winked. "I'm bad at math and good at immortality. You'll get used to it."

Tavi smelled faintly of synthetic strawberries and copper—like candy with teeth. Her eyes, bright gray with flecks of red, shimmered under the sun filtering in through the stairwell window.

"Please tell me you're not joining this investigation," Nyla said.

"Oh, absolutely I am." Tavi grinned, sharp canines flashing for half a heartbeat. "You need me. Ardelia said, and I quote, 'Take someone who can pass for human and not terrify baristas.'"

Kian raised a brow. "She sent her."

"She *volunteered*," Nyla corrected. "The Maestra said yes because she doesn't like arguing with glitter."

"Who does?" Tavi chirped. "Anyway, I'm your sunshine. Literally. You two get woozy above UV index five, I keep my tan."

"You're not supposed to *enjoy* it," Nyla muttered, descending the stairs.

"I enjoy everything," Tavi said. "You'd think 200 years of being 21 would kill enthusiasm, but nope. Eternal youth, baby."

Kian followed them down, shaking his head. "You ever grow tired of pretending?"

"Oh, I *am* tired," Tavi said. "Just not bored."

The air changed as they descended—the chill of subterranean soundproofing and the faint copper tang of preserved blood. The club's archives weren't glamorous: rows of shelves, analog decks, reels labeled in looping handwriting that belonged to DJs long dead or pretending not to be. The walls were layered with padded foam, and faint hums flickered through the space, like sleeping frequencies.

Nyla trailed her fingers along the spines of old vinyl sleeves, murmuring to herself as if reading the grooves by touch.

"House of Sound, pre-urbanization," she said softly. "This one's from before Miami was Miami."

Kian crouched near a crate, examining a tangled mess of cables. "You weren't kidding about ancient tech. Half of this should be in a museum."

"It is," Nyla said. "We just don't let the humans visit."

Tavi was already rummaging through a side cabinet, humming to herself. "You know, some of these recordings are locked. Like, actually locked. Who locks music?"

"People who remember what it can do," Nyla said. She reached for a box marked *AURAL TEMPLES: PRIVATE—ARCHIVE SEVEN.* The wax seal shimmered with faint red sigils.

Kian glanced at it. "Encrypted."

"I can open it."

"I figured."

She slid her pendant between her fingers and pressed it to the seal. The sigils responded instantly, flaring bright, then unraveling like film catching light. The box opened with a sigh that wasn't air.

Inside were a dozen reel-to-reel tapes, each labeled with a symbol—a spiral, a sunburst, a crescent wave. Old House notation.

"Looks like ritual recordings," Kian murmured.

"They are," Nyla said. "Siren prototypes. When resonance was still being tamed."

Tavi crouched beside them, eyes wide. "Wait, you mean the songs that—"

"Yes," Nyla interrupted. "The ones that broke cities."

Kian adjusted one of the reels, careful not to touch the magnetized surface. "Why keep them here?"

"Because Ardelia doesn't destroy history," Nyla said. "She buries it under better soundproofing."

Something about the air felt heavier now. Not dangerous yet, just… awake.

Nyla threaded one of the reels into the old playback deck. The motor whirred reluctantly, like an animal being coaxed out of sleep. She turned the gain low, just enough to catch whatever lingered.

Tavi flopped onto a beanbag chair, legs crossed, sipping from a thermos of deep red liquid through a straw. "Ooh, vintage. What year?"

"Don't joke," Kian said, watching the dials. "This isn't nostalgia. It's archaeology."

The tape hissed. Then—a sound.

Not music at first. More like a breath caught between oceans. Then a hum, deeper than any sub-bass, rising slow as sunrise through the floor. The room vibrated, subtle but insistent, like a heartbeat through water.

Nyla froze. Every cell in her body leaned forward. The resonance wasn't external—it was *inside her*. Her blood felt as though it had turned to light and sound at once. The pendant burned against her throat.

"Kill it," Kian said, already moving to the switch.

"Wait," Nyla breathed.

The hum turned to a chord. The chord opened into something older than language—notes that felt spoken into her spine, ancient vowels resonating where thought began. The air thickened with memory. The walls pulsed once.

Then a voice—low, and not one of theirs—cut through the frequency like thunder under velvet: "The Prime Note awakens."

The tape deck snapped silent. Every bulb in the archive flickered and went out.

For a moment, there was nothing but breathing. Nyla's, sharp and shallow. Kian's, steady but louder than it should have been.

Tavi broke the silence first. "Okay," she whispered. "So... either that was an audio glitch, or we just resurrected a myth."

Kian's jaw clenched. "Prime Note. That's a House legend."

"It's not a legend," Nyla said, voice distant. Her pulse was still trying to catch up with the echo inside her veins. "It's a warning."

Tavi blinked. "A warning about what?"

"Not what," Nyla murmured, staring at the dead reel. "Who."

Kian stepped closer, his voice low, almost reverent. "You heard it, didn't you?"

Nyla looked up at him. "I didn't just hear it," she said, eyes bright with something that looked almost like fear. "It heard me back."

The silence that followed wasn't the comfortable kind. It was the kind that pressed against your teeth, the kind that had a heartbeat.

Kian reached for the light switch. "Power cut?"

The bulbs above them flickered again—one, then three—trying to come back, but each pulse dimmed the room further, like the dark preferred itself.

Tavi sat up, thermos forgotten. "Uh... is anyone else's skin buzzing?"

"Yes," Nyla whispered. "Don't move."

Her pendant still glowed faintly, the same color as cooled metal. She touched it and winced. It was vibrating—not wildly, not dangerously—just enough to mimic a pulse that wasn't hers.

Kian leaned toward the reel deck. The tape wasn't spinning, but the reels twitched on their own, the way eyelids do in a bad dream.

"Turn it off," Nyla said, already backing up.

"It *is* off," he replied.

"No, it's *playing* something," she said. "I can still feel it."

The hum returned—not from the speakers, but from the concrete under their feet. The air got colder. The hair on Kian's arms stood up. From somewhere deep in the building came a second vibration, slower, heavier, like a subwoofer the size of the earth clearing its throat.

Tavi whimpered, "I—uh—I think I'd like to go back to the part of eternity where things made sense."

Then the tape began to unspool.

No power. No motor. Just movement. The magnetic ribbon peeled itself out of the reel, looping through the air like a ribbon underwater. It shimmered faintly—symbols glowing on its surface for a moment before fading.

Nyla's hunger roared awake. Not the kind she could feed with joy or pain, but the ancient kind—the blood-deep yearning the Houses had bred out generations ago. The song was *calling* her.

"Don't touch it," Kian said.

But she already had.

The floating strip brushed her fingertips, and the world convulsed.

She saw it—not a memory, not a vision, but an *impression.* A city built of sound. Not Miami. Older. Its skyline was columns of singing crystal; its streets shimmered with molten gold that pulsed like veins. Vampires walked among mortals openly there—radiant, unashamed, voices tuned to the earth's pitch. And above it all stood a figure cloaked in shadow, face blurred by light, mouth open in an endless note that cracked the sky itself.

Her pendant screamed—if metal could scream—and the vision snapped.

Nyla staggered backward, slamming against a shelf hard enough to rattle the records. Kian caught her before she hit the floor.

"Talk to me," he said, gripping her shoulders. "Nyla—what did you see?"

She could barely get the words out. "A city. Singing. And someone… someone watching through me."

The hum died. The tape fell to the floor like dead skin.

For a second, nothing moved.

Then every reel on the shelves began to spin—slowly, lazily, their spindles whining as if stirred from centuries of sleep. A thousand songs waking at once. The sound was faint, but underneath it came something new: a whisper threaded between frequencies.

Tavi clamped her hands over her ears. "It's *saying my name.*"

"It's not saying yours," Nyla murmured, eyes wide. "It's saying mine."

Kian bent, grabbing the fallen tape, and as soon as his fingers touched it, the spinning stopped. Every reel froze mid-turn. Silence returned, heavy and absolute.

He exhaled. "They're keyed to you."

"No," Nyla said, her voice shaking in a way she hated. "They're keyed to something *in* me."

Kian met her gaze, calm and steady but a shade paler than usual. "The Prime Note. It didn't awaken. It *recognized* you."

From the far corner of the archive, one of the old speakers crackled to life—faint, broken. And then, in that same impossible voice that had whispered through the reel, came five words that froze all three of them in place: "Welcome back to the song."

The power surged. Every bulb in the room flared white.

And somewhere deep beneath Midnight Tempo, something *answered back.*

# VII

The night broke open like glass.

Nyla heard it before the news broke—an absence that sliced through the city's noise like someone had reached out and pressed "mute" on life itself. The cars still moved, the surf still struck the pier, but the resonance—the faint thrum that every vampire felt in their marrow—was gone.

Something had emptied it.

By the time she and Kian reached the rival club, *The Vessel,* police lights pulsed against rain-slick concrete. Human officers stood outside the cordon, confused, anxious, none of them realizing what kind of crime scene they guarded. The tape fluttered. The air behind it trembled with the weight of things it couldn't explain.

Tavi was already there, perched on the hood of a squad car, her glitter sneakers swinging. She looked impossibly young, as always, but her usual grin had curdled at the edges.

"You don't want to go in there," she said quietly.

Nyla ducked under the tape anyway. "I never do."

Inside, *The Vessel* smelled wrong. Not like blood or death—but like a vacuum. Every sound she made felt swallowed. Her footsteps didn't echo. Her breathing seemed too shallow. Even the hum of electricity had vanished.

Bodies lay scattered near the stage, frozen mid-motion. One woman had her mouth open in a scream that hadn't escaped. A man still held a drink, liquid trembling at the rim, not from movement but from the faint vibration trying to fill the silence.

Kian stood beside one of the victims, his expression unreadable. "They're drained," he said.

"Of what?" Tavi asked. "There's no blood."

"Not blood," Nyla murmured, crouching. "Sound."

Kian nodded. "Resonance."

Tavi frowned. "How can you drain sound from someone who's already dead? That's, like, double-dead."

Nyla's eyes were fixed on the nearest body. "No, she's right. The dead are quiet—but they're not silent. A corpse hums at thirty-two hertz for three days after death. It's faint, but it's there. That's why we can tell when someone's been turned—when the hum changes pitch."

Kian's voice was low. "These don't hum at all."

She touched the woman's wrist. Nothing. No hum. No residual frequency. No trace of life or death. It was like touching stone.

It wasn't absence—it was *erasure.*

"Someone took everything," Nyla said. "The resonance, the frequency, the echo of who they were. There's nothing left to read."

Kian scanned the room, eyes tracing the shattered speakers, the warped mixer, the cracked ceiling. "They weren't killed for blood. They were silenced."

"Silence doesn't do this," Nyla said. "They keep their kills clean."

"They used to," Kian said.

That tone made her pause. "What do you mean *used to*?"

He didn't answer. Not immediately. He moved to the stage, where the club's DJ booth sat blackened by an electrical burn. His hand skimmed the melted edges of the equipment. The air around him rippled faintly, the way heat distorts asphalt.

Tavi stayed by the door, arms folded tight. "I hate this," she whispered. "The air feels wrong. Like it's thick with *no*."

"Go wait outside," Nyla said.

"I'm not leaving you."

"This isn't bravado, Tavi. You're half-human. You shouldn't be here."

"Newsflash: so is he," Tavi said, nodding toward Kian.

Nyla turned sharply. "What?"

Kian didn't look up from the console. "She's right."

Nyla blinked. "You're joking."

"No." He straightened, meeting her eyes. The light caught in them differently now—too still, too focused. "I'm not House-born. I was made."

Tavi's mouth fell open. "Wait, made how? Like, Ikea-made? Or—"

"House of Silence," Kian said simply. "My mother was human. My father was one of theirs."

The words landed heavy. The kind of revelation that rewired air.

Nyla stepped closer. "You're telling me you're *Silence.* That you've been working for them."

"I was trained by them," Kian said. "There's a difference."

"Explain it."

He leaned against the console, folding his arms. "The House of Silence has been breeding hybrids for over a century. Not vampires. Not mortals. Resonance-nullifiers. People who can walk between frequencies, immune to siren calls. We're meant to monitor the other Houses—contain them if they break code. If the music gets too loud."

"You're a weapon," Nyla said softly.

"I'm a firewall," Kian corrected. "They call us Dampers. Half human, half void."

Tavi wrinkled her nose. "That sounds like a terrible album title."

He ignored her. "I was assigned to the House of Sound six months ago. Observe, report, neutralize if necessary. But I didn't expect..." He gestured around the club, the bodies, the silence that felt heavier than gravity. "This."

"So you're a spy," Nyla said, voice sharp enough to cut through the static air.

"I was," he said. "Until last night."

She crossed her arms. "What changed?"

"You," he said simply.

Her jaw tightened. "Flattery won't save you."

"It's not flattery. It's fact." He took a slow step closer. "When you fed at that rooftop, I felt your pull. I should've been immune. Instead, I *heard* something. A sound under your sound. I think you woke whatever's been sleeping beneath Miami."

Nyla stared at him. "You think I started this?"

"I think you triggered it," Kian said. "The Prime Note. The hum that's supposed to stay buried."

Tavi raised her hand. "Okay, pause. Can someone explain to the glitter person what a Prime Note is before I implode?"

Nyla exhaled, turning toward her. "The Prime Note is the first sound the Houses ever recorded. The vibration that split our kind from the human line. It's what gave us resonance—what let us feed without blood. The Maestra says it's mythical. A story to keep fledglings humble."

Kian shook his head. "It's not a myth. It's a frequency buried under the city, locked by the founding Houses. If it wakes, it can rewrite the balance between us."

"And now people are dying," Nyla said.

"Not dying," Kian corrected quietly. "Being rewritten."

That landed like thunder.

She crouched beside another body—a man in a suit, expensive, cold. His mouth was open, but his throat looked unmarked. When she brushed her fingers along his jaw, a static shock jumped between them. Her skin prickled. For half a second, she heard something—like a word echoing inside her skull, not in English but in pitch.

She flinched back.

Kian was beside her instantly. "What did you hear?"

"Not hear," she said, shaking her head. "*Feel.* It said—" She stopped. The memory wasn't sound. It was texture. "It said… 'borrowed.'"

Tavi's voice trembled. "Borrowed what?"

Nyla looked up, eyes bright with something fierce and terrible. "Us."

Outside, a police radio crackled, then went dead. The hum of the city faltered again—small things first: traffic sounds dampened, the sea's roar softened, even the breeze seemed to lose its music.

Kian moved to the window. His reflection didn't move with him. The glass didn't echo him back.

He swore under his breath. "It's spreading."

Nyla's hunger flared—a survival instinct when the world went quiet. "We need to get out of here."

Tavi didn't move. She was staring at the victims. "They look peaceful."

"That's not peace," Nyla said, taking her arm. "That's void."

When they stepped back into the street, the silence followed them out like a shadow. It was quieter than the grave but louder than thought. Every vampire on the block could feel it—the ache in the teeth, the pressure behind the eyes.

Tavi winced. "My fillings are humming."

"It's the residue," Kian said. "Every living frequency in a one-mile radius is off by two hertz. You'll feel it until you leave the district."

Nyla turned to him. "You sound like you've seen this before."

"I have," he said. "Once. In Havana, 1962. A resonance collapse. Forty-three dead. We thought we contained it. We were wrong."

"So why didn't you tell me who you were?"

"Would you have trusted me?"

"No," she admitted. "But I wouldn't have liked you any less."

That surprised him. "You like me now?"

"I like that you keep saving my life," she said. "But I still don't know which side you're on."

"I don't either," he said quietly.

Tavi blew out a shaky breath. "Okay, team therapy's cute, but maybe we should tell Ardelia that her city's going mute?"

"No," Nyla said. "Not yet. If the Council finds out there's a Silence hybrid in her House, they'll execute both of you before breakfast."

"Then what do we do?"

Nyla looked back at the club, its windows dark and open-mouthed. "We follow the hum."

Kian frowned. "There is no hum."

"There's always a hum," she said. "You just have to know where to listen."

For a long beat, the three of them just stood there in the wet, broken silence outside *The Vessel.* The air was thick with something that wasn't quite wind, a low static whisper threading between passing cars and the faint hiss of a neon sign that refused to die.

Nyla tilted her head slightly, closing her eyes. The world looked different when you stopped hearing it like a human. She let her breath flatten, steady. The noise of Miami—horns, sirens, distant laughter—peeled back layer by layer until only the residual vibration remained: the city's pulse, deep and endless. Somewhere beneath that was something else—an unsteady rhythm like a drum with a tear in its skin. It wasn't gone yet. It was moving.

"I've got it," she murmured.

Kian frowned. "Got what?"

"The echo. It's not random. It's traveling along the fiber grid—through the power lines, maybe even the water mains."

He blinked at her. "You can hear that?"

"Not with my ears." She tapped the side of her neck, just above the collarbone, where the faint outline of a vein pulsed in time with something deeper. "With this."

Tavi squinted at her. "Please don't tell me your neck can do Wi-Fi now."

"It's resonance," Kian said before Nyla could respond. "She's following the leftover frequency."

Nyla opened her eyes. "It's faint, but it's there. The same kind of hum that came from the rooftop before the glass turned on me. It's pulling east."

"East is the water," Kian said, already checking his watch like the hour mattered.

"Exactly." She started walking. "Whatever's using these frequencies—it's not just bouncing them off surfaces. It's *channeling* them. Like the bay's a giant tuning fork."

Tavi groaned, trotting to catch up. "Fantastic. So we're chasing ghost music now? Because that's my favorite kind of horror."

No one laughed.

As they crossed Collins Avenue, the usual noise of the city began to dull. Not fade—compress. Like the world was inhaling and forgot how to exhale. The closer they got to the shoreline, the more distorted things became. Streetlights flickered in synchronized pulses. A dog barked, but the echo lagged by two beats. Even the waves, when they hit the seawall, made no real sound—just the faint hiss of displaced air.

Nyla paused under a flickering lamp, eyes narrowing. "Feel that?"

Kian touched the pole with two fingers. The metal trembled. "The current's dirty. Not electric—something piggybacking on the charge."

"Sound doesn't piggyback," Tavi said.

"This does," Nyla replied. "It's like the city's bones are carrying someone else's heartbeat."

She kept walking, boots splashing through shallow puddles, the neon reflections quivering in distorted reds and blues. Kian followed, silent now, scanning rooftops, the drain grates, the sky—anything that could act as a conductor.

"Where's it strongest?" he asked.

Nyla stopped in the middle of an empty intersection, hands out like she could feel the air the way blind men feel walls. Her pendant vibrated faintly. "Downhill."

"The waterfront," Kian said again, softer this time—less as a direction, more as a confirmation of dread.

Tavi's breath fogged the air. "You two are creeping me out."

"Good," Nyla said. "Means we're getting closer."

She started moving faster, cutting between shuttered storefronts and graffiti-covered delivery trucks. The further east they went, the colder it felt, despite the Florida heat. The humidity had teeth now.

Kian fell into step beside her. "How do you stand it?"

"The hum?" she asked.

He nodded.

"It's not pain," she said after a moment. "It's hunger shaped like music."

"That's worse."

She didn't argue.

The hum strengthened as they neared the docks. It wasn't audible to human ears—it lived somewhere just below consciousness, like the pull of the tide inside the skull. Nyla's pulse aligned with it until she could feel her own heartbeat syncing to the city's, the two rhythms slowly braiding together.

By the time the water came into view, the silence had changed again. It wasn't empty anymore. It was waiting.

And that's when Kian realized they weren't chasing the hum.

It was leading them.

They followed it to the waterfront.

At first glance, the bay looked normal—sailboats bobbing, joggers running the pier, music drifting faintly from nearby bars. But to Nyla, the whole city sounded *off-key.*

She closed her eyes and let her senses stretch. Beneath the surface of the water, something thrummed. Faint. Distant. Not natural.

"I can feel it," she murmured.

Kian nodded. "It's the same frequency as the archive recording."

"You sure?"

He gestured to the metal railing. "Touch it."

She did—and nearly recoiled. The steel pulsed with soundless rhythm. It wasn't vibration, exactly. It was memory. She could *taste* it—copper, static, the ghost of applause.

"It's feeding through the water," she said. "Traveling by reflection. The bay acts like an amplifier."

Kian glanced at her pendant. "Your resonance is the key. That's why it reacts to you. Why it called you Prime."

"I didn't ask to be a tuning fork for ancient disasters."

"No one ever asks," he said.

Tavi leaned on the railing, eyes wide. "So let me get this straight: some ancient mixtape of doom is leaking through the bay, rewriting vampires into paperweights, and our best defense is the girl who accidentally woke it up?"

"Essentially," Kian said.

"Well, fantastic." She grinned weakly. "No pressure."

"None at all," Nyla said. "But we need to know who's using it."

She turned back toward the skyline. Somewhere beyond those towers, the Houses were already whispering—accusations, theories, fears. She could almost hear them, if she listened hard enough.

Someone had resurrected the Prime Note. Someone who knew how to weaponize resonance.

Kian's voice broke her thoughts. "If we go any deeper, you'll need protection. The next wave could hit before we detect it."

"I have you," she said.

"You have a liability with a complicated family tree."

"Same thing."

For a heartbeat, his expression softened. "Nyla, if you get too close—if it reaches through you again—you might not come back as yourself."

She stepped closer, lowering her voice. "Then you'll pull me back."

"I might not be able to."

"Try harder," she said.

The water shimmered beneath them, and for the first time, Kian looked genuinely afraid.

He turned away, resting both palms on the rail. The faint hum resonated up his arms. His eyes darkened—not just in color, but depth. "You don't understand what it means to be half Silence. I can *feel* when the void starts listening. It's listening now."

She reached out, fingers brushing his wrist. "Then talk louder."

Tavi groaned. "I swear, if you two start flirting while the apocalypse hums in stereo—"

But then the pier itself quivered. A tremor shot through the ground, small but undeniable. The bay went still—mirror-flat—and from the distance came a low, rolling tone.

It wasn't thunder.

It was music.

Only it didn't belong to any of them.

The sound crawled under their skin, pulling at bone, at blood, until Nyla gasped. She felt her resonance bend, the Prime Note in her veins answering like a dog to its master.

Kian stepped between her and the water, pressing his palm against her chest—not hard, just enough to ground her. "Stay with me."

"It's calling," she said, voice thin. "It wants—"

He shook his head. "No. It wants *in*."

Tavi took a step back, eyes wide. "It's spreading again."

The lights along the pier flickered, one by one, until only their reflections remained. Somewhere behind them, alarms wailed across the city—fire, police, everything—but even those began to distort, twisting into an atonal drone.

Kian tightened his grip on Nyla. "We have to go."

"I can stop it," she whispered. "If I find the source."

"You can't even stand straight."

"Then you hold me steady."

"Nyla—"

"Trust me."

He looked at her—really looked—and for a moment, she saw the war inside him: Silence and Sound, human and monster, duty and choice. Then he nodded once. "You get one chance."

She turned her face toward the bay, closed her eyes, and reached.

The hum surged, and the world tilted. For a heartbeat, she felt every living frequency in the city—their heartbeats, their conversations, their songs, their fears. It was intoxicating, terrifying. She could feel the Prime Note vibrating inside her, calling its siblings to wake.

And beneath it all, another voice—cold, patient, waiting.

**"Find me, Nyla Voss. Finish the chord."**

Her eyes snapped open, glowing faintly in the dark.

Kian caught her as her knees buckled. "What did it say?"

She swallowed hard, trembling. "It has a name."

Tavi leaned in. "What name?"

Nyla's lips parted, and the word came out barely audible—a sound and a wound at once. "*Almany.*"

The water rippled at the word, light bending, as if the city itself recognized it. And in that moment, they all knew—Miami was no longer theirs.

# VIII

The summons arrived at dusk, printed on glass.

That was how the House preferred it—dramatic, precise, impossible to ignore. The translucent sheet shimmered with Ardelia's sigil, its lines pulsing faintly in Nyla's hand like veins of light. *Council Convocation, 8:00 p.m., Studio A.*

When the Maestra called a convocation, no one declined. Not even the ones she'd raised to believe they didn't kneel.

By the time Nyla stepped into the atrium of Arista House Records, the building no longer looked like a label. The lobby had been stripped of its day veneer—no interns, no potted plants, no music leaking from the demo rooms. Just silence and formality. The elders had arrived.

They stood in small clusters: Resonants draped in silks that moved like liquid sound, faces sharp with power. Each represented a House cell—New Orleans, São

Paulo, Kingston, Madrid. Most eyed Nyla as she entered, their expressions balancing curiosity with quiet accusation.

Marisol caught her near the stairs. "Don't rise to it," she murmured. "They're waiting for you to."

"Good to know I'm everyone's favorite suspect," Nyla said, forcing a smirk.

"Not favorite," Marisol said. "Convenient."

The double doors to Studio A opened without touch. Ardelia stood at the head of the long obsidian table, flanked by two Council envoys in white—symbol of neutrality, though nothing about them ever was.

"Nyla Voss," Ardelia said, voice carrying the kind of weight that made mortals confess. "Come forward."

Nyla obeyed, spine straight, face unreadable. The murmurs quieted, leaving only the low buzz of power—like distant thunder trapped in glass.

Ardelia's gaze swept the room. "You've all seen the reports. Two resonance collapses in less than a week. One confirmed fatal. The other—last night—contained before escalation."

"She contained it," Marisol interjected before anyone else could. "Saved half the pier."

A woman near the far end scoffed. "Or caused it."

"She's right," said another. "Every incident traces back to her sets. The frequencies spike, the city trembles, people die without blood left to hum."

"That's enough," Ardelia said, not raising her voice but cutting through theirs all the same. "Speculation helps no one."

A thin man in gray leaned forward, eyes like unpolished steel. "Maestra, you protect her because she's yours. But this is beyond a technical glitch. The Prime Note is not a myth. We all felt the tremor under the bay. Someone woke it."

Nyla's pulse jumped. "And you think that someone is me?"

The man didn't answer, which was worse than yes.

Ardelia stepped between them, the hem of her robe whispering across the floor. "Nyla's work keeps this House relevant. The Prime Note has been legend for centuries. None of us know if it truly exists."

"But *she* heard it," another Resonant said. "And after she did, the silence spread."

Nyla could feel the room leaning in, like a pack scenting blood—or fear. She kept her chin high. "You want a villain. Fine. But I was at the scene last night. Ask your own data techs—my resonance output was steady. Someone else is orchestrating this."

"And who would dare?" the man in gray asked.

"Silence," Nyla said simply. "Or someone working with them."

That stirred the room into uneasy murmurs. The Houses had feuded before, but accusing another of weaponizing resonance was close to blasphemy.

Ardelia let the voices rise, then cut them down with one word. "Enough."

Her tone carried a command older than the city. Even the air obeyed.

"We will not descend into paranoia," she said, sweeping her gaze across the assembly. "The House of Sound survives because we hold discipline where others hold fear. I will investigate personally. Until then, no member of this House will accuse another."

It was a performance, and she knew Nyla knew it.

Ardelia turned, voice gentling by degrees. "Nyla, you will remain under my supervision. No performances. No contact with the Council. I'll handle the politics."

Nyla bowed her head slightly, the gesture more habit than submission. "Yes, Maestra."

The meeting dissolved into uneasy goodbyes. One by one, the Resonants drifted out—leaving behind the faint echo of their distrust, an aftertaste in the air Nyla could practically bite.

When the last door closed, Ardelia exhaled. "You're lucky I still have a few friends on that Council."

"Friends or debts?"

"Both," Ardelia said, moving toward the console. "They wanted to strip your title tonight. Claim you're unstable."

"I'm not."

"Then convince me."

The words were soft, but they landed hard.

Nyla crossed her arms. "You think I'm losing control."

"I think something inside you is changing," Ardelia said. "And I can't decide if it's a gift or a curse."

"The Prime Note," Nyla said. "You knew it wasn't a myth."

Ardelia didn't deny it. She adjusted one of the console's dials, though no sound played. "I've heard fragments. Whispers in recordings older than the archives. We all have."

"You didn't tell me."

"It wasn't your burden to carry."

"Then whose is it?" Nyla snapped. "Because it feels like mine."

Ardelia's eyes softened, but her voice stayed cold. "If you lose control—if you become the breach—I'll end it myself. Cleanly. With honor."

For a heartbeat, neither spoke. The air between them hummed—not threat, not affection, but inevitability.

"You'd kill me," Nyla said quietly.

"I'd protect the House," Ardelia replied. "Even from you."

The honesty hurt more than the warning.

Nyla took a step closer. "You're not telling me everything."

"No one ever tells everything," Ardelia said, turning away. "That's how we survive."

Nyla wanted to argue. She wanted to accuse. But something in Ardelia's tone—almost mournful—stopped her.

Instead, she asked the question she shouldn't have. "How did you first hear it?"

Ardelia froze. Her reflection in the dark glass of the studio window didn't move with her. When she spoke, her voice was almost a whisper. "Once, before you were born, the city trembled like it did last night. The Council buried it. They said it was a resonance quake. I knew better."

"You heard the Prime Note."

"I heard something that pretended to be."

Nyla's skin prickled. "And what happened?"

Ardelia turned back to her. "An entire district went silent for a week. No music. No speech. Just... hush. When the sound returned, three of my Resonants were gone. No bodies. No hum. Nothing."

"Erased," Nyla murmured.

"Yes." Ardelia's expression hardened again. "I swore it would never happen again."

"And yet here we are."

"Here we are," Ardelia echoed.

A low vibration crawled through the floor, so faint most wouldn't notice. But they both felt it.

Nyla looked down, then back up. "That's not me."

Ardelia nodded once. "I know."

"Then what is it?"

"An invitation," Ardelia said. "Someone—or something—is calling the Prime Note home."

Nyla took a breath that trembled. "And you think it wants me."

"I think it's already inside you," Ardelia said softly. "The question is whether you'll conduct it… or be consumed by it."

Outside, thunder rolled—no storm, just pressure. Miami's skyline hummed in the distance, low and discordant. The Prime Note was no longer legend.

It was warming up.

Nyla stayed where she was long after the thunder faded, her reflection caught in the glass beside Ardelia's. Two silhouettes—teacher and student, monster and heir.

Behind the mirrored surface, the city glittered like a living thing, unaware it was sitting atop the corpse of another.

"Why didn't they destroy it?" she asked finally, her voice smaller than she meant it to be.

Ardelia didn't answer right away. She traced the rim of a crystal glass with one long finger. It made no sound.

"The Prime Note was our genesis," she said at last. "The first resonance. Before blood, before thirst. It was the sound that separated us from what we used to be. Some believed it was divine—others, a mistake."

Nyla frowned. "And which are we?"

"That depends who you ask." Ardelia's mouth curved, not quite a smile. "The old Houses called it *The Fracture.* They said the Prime Note wasn't created. It escaped."

"Escaped from what?"

"The human ear," Ardelia said softly. "Once, it lived inside them—every heartbeat, every song. When the Fracture came, the Note slipped free. It found us, the ones already half between worlds. We learned to feed on what it left behind."

Nyla absorbed that quietly. It wasn't the first time she'd heard bits of the myth, but coming from Ardelia, it felt heavier. Realer. Like memory disguised as story.

"And now it wants back in," she murmured.

"Perhaps," Ardelia said. "Or perhaps it's simply tired of sleeping."

Nyla turned from the window. "If you believed it was just a story, why bury the recordings? Why teach us to fear silence?"

Ardelia's eyes flicked toward her. "Because silence listens. Because every frequency carries a memory of what came before, and if we're careless, it remembers how to answer."

The Maestra stepped closer, lowering her voice. "The Prime Note was supposed to be locked beneath the city when the first Houses were founded. The Council used a triad seal—Sound, Silence, and Stone. It held for centuries. But something's weakening it. Maybe the storms. Maybe us."

"Maybe both," Nyla said. "Maybe every song we've ever played was one more knock on the door."

Ardelia studied her, and for the first time, Nyla saw genuine weariness in her eyes. "You're not wrong. Each generation gets louder. We call it evolution. Maybe it's erosion."

A quiet laugh escaped Nyla—small, humorless. "So what now? You keep pretending to protect me while planning how to kill me just in case?"

"If I were planning to kill you, I wouldn't be warning you," Ardelia said. "You'd never hear it coming."

That earned a thin smile from Nyla. "Comforting."

"Necessary."

Nyla turned her gaze back to the city. Somewhere out there, the hum was threading through steel and water, finding new places to hide. She could almost feel it under her skin, a faint vibration that refused to fade.

Ardelia's voice softened again. "When I first heard it, I thought it was beautiful. I wanted to believe the Note was calling us home. But beauty can be cruel, Nyla. Music kills more efficiently than fire if you play it wrong."

"I don't intend to play it wrong," Nyla said.

"No one does," Ardelia murmured. "That's why I'm afraid."

The Maestra reached out, brushing Nyla's cheek—not a caress, more like a benediction. "Whatever you are becoming, hold on to the part that still listens to mercy. The Prime Note doesn't understand it."

Nyla nodded once, uncertain she believed mercy had anything left to do with her.

When she finally left the room, Ardelia's reflection stayed behind in the glass—staring into the city as if she could already see the cracks forming beneath the surface, humming quietly to herself a song too old to be safe.

# IX

The drive out to Kian's studio was quiet in the way long nights are after too many questions.
Miami blurred past in muted neon; the streets were half empty, the horizon bruised violet where the water met sky.

Kian didn't say much, and Nyla didn't push. His silences had gravity—heavy, but not cold. They filled a room the way bass filled a song.

When they finally stopped, the air felt different. Cleaner, thinner. The building was a warehouse tucked behind a row of forgotten murals, the kind of place that used to store art before art went digital. He keyed open a side door, and the quiet inside felt unnatural—suffocating even.

"This is where you disappear when you're not saving me from myself?" she asked, stepping inside.

He flipped on a low strip of lighting. "It's where I keep the things I can't explain."

The space wasn't large, but it was meticulous: brushed concrete floors, panels lined with acoustic foam, an array of instruments and equipment that looked equal parts science and religion. At the far end, behind reinforced glass, a sealed chamber hummed faintly—soundproof, but not silent.

Nyla moved toward it instinctively. "What is that?"

"My insurance policy," he said. "The Council calls it a counterfrequency stabilizer. I call it a mistake I can't unmake."

She turned to face him. "You built a weapon."

"I built a mirror," Kian corrected. "If you or anyone like you loses control, this—" he gestured to the chamber "—finds the exact opposite vibration and fires it back. It cancels everything. Even resonance."

She raised an eyebrow. "So, it kills us."

"If you're feeding recklessly, yes. But it's meant for containment, not execution."

Nyla walked the perimeter of the chamber, her pendant vibrating faintly as she neared it. "And you trust yourself to use it?"

"I trust my intentions," he said. "The rest depends on who I'm standing in front of."

Their eyes met, and something unsaid sparked between them—equal parts challenge and invitation.

Nyla tilted her head, smiling just enough to be dangerous. "Then show me."

Kian hesitated. "You don't want that."

"Maybe I do." She stepped closer, her voice low, almost melodic. "You said you were immune. Prove it."

He exhaled, running a hand through his hair. "You're not going to like how it feels."

"Neither will you," she murmured.

He adjusted a dial on the console. The lights dimmed, a soft red glow bleeding through the walls. "When I say stop, you stop."

"Don't give orders you can't enforce," she said.

And then she sang.

Not with words—just tone. A vibration that filled the air like heated honey, sweet and slow. The studio responded instantly; lights flickered, the panels shivered, every object caught the frequency and held it. It wasn't loud, but it was consuming.

Kian took a step forward into it. Most people would have swayed, dizzy from her pull. He didn't. He let it wash over him, body tensing against it like a man standing in a storm.

His voice cut through the sound, low and steady. "You're testing your limit, not mine."

She smiled. "I haven't even started."

He reached to the control panel and pressed a key. A wave of counterfrequency rolled through the room—a pulse of clean air that sliced her tone in half. The energy hit her chest like a heartbeat out of sync.

Nyla gasped. "You—"

He turned the dial again, and the silence that followed wasn't emptiness—it was resistance. Every molecule of sound she created dissolved before it reached him. It was infuriating, impossible, and exhilarating all at once.

"You can't silence me," she said, trying to push through it.

"I can," he said, voice softer now, closer. "But I won't."

The space between them grew smaller. Her resonance fought his calm, the two waves colliding until the air itself vibrated. She could feel his pulse against hers, that impossible mix of quiet and control, the place where her hunger met his restraint.

"You're not supposed to be able to do that," she whispered.

"Maybe I'm not supposed to want to," he said.

Something in her cracked open then—not the kind of break that hurt, but the kind that let light in.

She reached for him, one hand at his throat, the other over his heart, and let the sound pour from her—not song, not feeding, just need made audible. The vibration rolled through him, through the walls, through everything, and still he stood there, holding her steady.

Their breaths tangled. The red light pulsed in time with her heartbeat.

"Tell me what you feel," she said, her voice shaking now.

"Everything," he said. "And nothing."

It wasn't a kiss—not exactly—but when she leaned in, the silence between them broke like a held note finally released.

She didn't mean to feed. It happened instinctively, a current drawn to grounding wire. Her resonance slipped through her lips and into him, tasting not like blood but like static and warmth and something impossibly human. It burned and soothed in the same breath.

For the first time in her life, feeding didn't quiet the hunger. It multiplied it. His immunity didn't block her; it reflected her back at herself, forcing her to taste her own ache.

She pulled away, shivering. "I can't—"

He caught her wrist, gentle but firm. "Then don't."

Her pulse stuttered against his fingers. "You don't understand. I'm not full."

He looked at her, steady and unflinching. "You're not supposed to be."

The words hit her harder than the silence.

Because he was right—feeding wasn't supposed to satisfy. It was supposed to connect. And in that moment, standing in a room built to erase sound, she had never felt more alive.

The hum faded. The lights steadied. They stood facing each other, breathing like survivors of a storm neither of them had intended to start.

Nyla reached up, brushing her thumb along his jaw. "You should be terrified of me."

"I am," Kian said. "That's why I keep coming back."

Outside, the night settled again. But somewhere beneath the city, deep under the bay, a low vibration answered her heartbeat—as if the Prime Note itself had felt her feed and was humming approval.

The silence afterward wasn't empty—it pulsed. Every breath between them felt amplified, hanging in the still air of the soundproof studio.

Nyla could still taste the resonance she'd drawn from him, electric and disorienting. Her body was caught between craving and recoil, her pulse stumbling through both at once. She wasn't used to being unsteady. She wasn't used to anyone holding still through her storm.

Kian hadn't moved. He was close enough for her to catch the scent of him—salt, ozone, and that faint trace of copper that lived in everyone who'd been touched by the Houses. His hands rested loosely at his sides, but his focus stayed on her, sharp and unflinching.

"What do you see when you look at me?" she asked, voice quieter than the hum beneath their feet.

He took a slow breath. "Something that should terrify me, but doesn't."

"Flattery again."

"No," he said. "Observation."

She stepped closer until the front of her jacket brushed his shirt. The movement was subtle, but the air shifted.

The entire room seemed to lean toward them, pulled by something neither of them was willing to name.

"You feed on silence," she said. "How does that work?"

He tilted his head slightly. "I don't feed on it. I make it."

"That's worse."

He almost smiled. "For who?"

"For me," she said, softer. "Because I can feel it now—your quiet—it's not nothing. It's *pressure.*"

Kian's gaze held hers. "You can stop if you want."

"Do I look like I want to stop?" she said, the question half challenge, half confession.

He moved then, closing the last inch between them. Not sudden—measured, like everything he did. His hand came up, fingers brushing the curve of her jaw. It wasn't control, not exactly, but calibration—testing how much of her the silence could hold before it shattered.

The air thickened, heavy with the low pulse of their mismatched heartbeats. Nyla's resonance pushed outward, instinctive, hungry for response. His silence pushed back, equal and opposite. The collision was friction—heat, charge, the unbearable sweetness of restraint.

"You're burning," he murmured.

"So stop me," she whispered.

"I'd have to touch you."

"That's the point."

He did.

His other hand found the small of her back, steadying her as the energy rolled through them both. Nyla inhaled sharply, the sound catching between a gasp and a laugh. She could feel his pulse against her palm—steady, human—and underneath it, the faintest ghost of that impossible void that made him what he was.

For a second, she let herself lean in.

The hum in the room changed key—higher, finer, until it wasn't sound anymore but sensation. The floor trembled beneath them. Her pendant glowed faintly, responding to the storm in her blood.

"You shouldn't be able to do that," he said against her temple.

"Neither should you," she murmured. "And yet here we are."

She wanted to taste him again, to see if the hunger would quiet this time, if feeding on something that couldn't break would finally fill the hollow inside her. But the thought scared her—how easy it would be to forget what she was, and how close he already stood to the edge.

Kian must have sensed it, because he pulled back first. His hands dropped from her skin but didn't retreat completely. "You felt it, didn't you? When you fed."

Nyla nodded, breath unsteady. "It wasn't blood. It was… everything. Every sound I've ever made coming back to me."

"And?"

"And I wanted more." Her eyes found his. "That's what frightens me."

He brushed a thumb along her wrist. "Then don't feed from me again."

She smiled faintly, though her voice trembled. "You make that sound easy."

"It isn't," he admitted. "But neither is staying alive."

They stood there in the half-dark, the room still vibrating with what they hadn't said. Somewhere deep in the walls, the counterfrequency stabilizer hummed softly, trying to return the world to equilibrium.

Nyla's voice broke the silence again, low and raw. "Every time I touch you, I hear something new."

"What do you hear now?" Kian asked.

Her answer was a whisper, but it carried all the weight in the world. "Myself."

She turned toward the door, the red light painting the outline of her hair in molten color. He didn't stop her. He didn't need to. The hum followed her out like a pulse she couldn't quite escape, her hunger and his silence still entangled in the air.

Beneath it all—barely audible, but there—the faintest tremor of the Prime Note, listening, learning, waiting for the next time they would break it together.

It started with a map that wasn't supposed to exist.

Three days after the pier tremor, Kian had gone silent—no messages, no signal—vanished into the grid like a ghost that finally remembered it was one. Ardelia's council had locked down every file connected to the Prime Note investigation, citing "containment protocols." Even Marisol avoided her eyes now, murmuring about safety and silence and the danger of knowing too much.

But Nyla had never been good at staying still.

The city itself seemed restless—frequencies overlapping, radios glitching to static mid-song, elevators humming half a key too low. Something under Miami was stirring, and the Maestra's measured calm only confirmed what Nyla already feared: the Council wasn't trying to stop the House of Silence. They were trying to negotiate with them.

She'd started digging the way she always did—alone, half fueled by defiance, half by instinct. The archives gave her nothing. But the city's forgotten corners still whispered if you knew how to ask. So she went where whispers gathered: old transmitters, burned-out substations, derelict studios that smelled of dust and secrets.

It was in one of those—an abandoned radio museum near Coral Way—that she found it.
A piece of paper that shouldn't have been paper at all, pressed between two shattered transmitter coils. When she unfolded it, the ink shimmered like wet oil, the kind that only appeared when exposed to a Resonant's touch.

It wasn't written language. It was *notation*—ancient sound script, the kind used before frequencies became words. But Nyla could read it. The Prime Note had changed something in her; the symbols didn't look foreign anymore. They looked *familiar*.

The pattern spiraled inward, ending in a symbol she recognized only from myth: a vertical line crossing a circle—House of Silence territory.

She stared at the address coordinates printed beneath the glyphs. The numbers led nowhere on any map, but when she cross-referenced them against decommissioned broadcast networks, one tower pinged—a dead signal just south of the bay. The Dead Beacon. A radio relay long stripped of function and memory.

She smiled despite herself. It was almost poetic—the people who worshipped quiet hiding inside the bones of what used to scream across the sky.

Ardelia would never sanction the intrusion. Kian would try to stop her. So Nyla didn't tell either of them. She packed light—hooded jacket, pendant, one flask—and drove out past the edge of the city until the skyline disappeared behind fog.

Every mile out, the hum beneath her ribs grew thinner, the air duller. It wasn't peace. It was *pressure.* The world itself holding its breath.

She parked in the overgrown field half a mile from the tower, listening to the static flicker faintly through her pendant. Her own resonance had started to distort the closer she came, skipping like a record. Even her voice, when she muttered a curse under her breath, came out hollow, as though it didn't belong to her.

Still, she walked on.

The Dead Beacon rose ahead—an iron skeleton clawing at the sky, its cables swaying in the wind like dying veins. The sound around it was wrong; the sea hissed somewhere nearby, but even the waves seemed afraid to crash too loudly.

It was beautiful in a way that frightened her: the kind of beauty that came from precision, from an entire place tuned to one impossible key.

That was when she felt it—that faint, deliberate pull beneath her feet. Not the hum she knew, but the *absence* of it. A vacuum so complete it sang.

And Nyla realized the coordinates weren't just directions. They were an invitation.

She pressed her palm against the cool metal frame of the tower and smiled, despite the ache building behind her eyes.

The trick to breaking into the House of Silence was remembering they didn't listen with ears.

Nyla waited until the hour between heartbeat and sunrise, when the city's pulse slowed just enough to hide her own. She left Kian asleep—if he even slept—and moved through the fog that clung to the edges of the bay, drawn by a hum so faint it barely existed.

Every vampire had a pitch: a frequency that betrayed them no matter how quiet they tried to be. But Silence didn't broadcast—it *absorbed*. The only way to hear them was to follow where the world went missing.

So, she listened for *absence*.

And that's how she found the tower.

It rose from the mangroves on the outskirts of the city, an iron skeleton left from the 1950s, long abandoned, its cables rusted into the soil. Locals called it the Dead Beacon. She could feel its hush from miles away—a hollow in the air, a place where even her own footsteps dulled.

No humans came here. Even the animals avoided it.

Nyla parked a mile out and crossed the field on foot, hoodie pulled low, every sense straining. Her pendant stayed cold, the silence around her dense enough to muffle breath. She should have turned back then. But the hum under her skin—the one that had been getting louder since she fed from Kian—guided her onward.

At the tower's base, the ground wasn't solid. It gave slightly under her boot. She knelt, brushing away dirt until she found the seam of a hatch. Old, industrial, locked with a simple magnetic seal that still thrummed faintly with power.

She pressed her pendant against it. The metal sighed open like it had been waiting.

A ladder descended into darkness.

She took it.

The air grew colder as she climbed. The deeper she went, the less sound existed. Not quiet—total *erasure.* Even her pulse dulled. When she exhaled, there was no breath to hear. It was like the air swallowed proof of her existence.

At the bottom, she found a tunnel lit by bioluminescent strips that pulsed faintly blue. Every vibration in her body screamed *wrong.*

The corridor opened into a cavern—massive, carved directly beneath the old tower. What had once been a radio relay chamber was now transformed into a temple of silence.

Hundreds of them knelt in concentric circles: pale figures in dark robes, motionless, heads bowed. Vampires—House of Silence. They didn't move, didn't breathe, but their presence pressed on her like gravity. The entire space thrummed with a low, steady pressure, the inverse of sound.

Nyla pressed herself against a steel column, barely daring to blink.

They weren't feeding on blood or resonance. They were feeding on *suppression itself.* The silence had substance—an energy that rolled in invisible waves from the meditating figures. It hit her body like cold water, pressing down on her resonance until it stuttered.

The more they fed, the dimmer the air became. Light seemed to dissolve against them.

In the center of the room, on a raised platform, stood a single figure—taller than the rest, cloaked in gray, face obscured. Their hands hovered above something—or someone—bound to the floor.

Nyla edged closer, each step deliberate, her senses screaming against the weight of the hush. When she finally saw what lay at the leader's feet, her stomach turned.

It was a Resonant. A vampire from her own House. His eyes were open but empty, pupils glassed over. His body jerked in shallow spasms, every muscle straining against invisible strings. A faint echo rippled from him—too faint to be life.

The leader's voice was barely more than breath, but it carried through the room like an idea.
"Release the excess. Starve the noise."

The kneeling figures lifted their heads in eerie synchrony. No sound. Just motion. And then—slowly, impossibly—the Resonant's skin began to pale, his veins turning black before fading completely.

They were *draining his resonance.*

Nyla's hand covered her mouth, though there was nothing left to stifle. The process wasn't violent; it was *careful.* Like a candle being snuffed.

When they were finished, the body didn't fall—it simply stopped being. Flesh without sound. Not dead, not alive—emptied.

The leader raised their head slightly, the hood shifting just enough for Nyla to glimpse a face that wasn't a face at all—smooth, translucent skin stretched over faint light.

"Another fracture mended," the voice murmured. "Soon there will be no House but Silence."

The words weren't heard—they arrived directly inside her head, vibrating behind her eyes.

Nyla stumbled back, heart racing in a room where hearts didn't. The movement sent a faint ripple through the air.

The leader's head snapped toward her.

She froze.

The silence deepened. Then, from somewhere across the chamber, a whisper—not hers—slid through her thoughts. "You don't belong here, daughter of sound."

Her pulse roared, a drumbeat in the void. They were *inside* her resonance now, crawling through her frequency.

Nyla bolted.

She didn't think—just ran. Her boots hit metal, her breath tearing from lungs that didn't dare make noise. The tunnel walls shook as the meditating vampires stirred, their collective focus snapping toward the disturbance.

The air thickened, her ears filling with pressure. Her vision tunneled. Every instinct screamed *too loud, too loud, too loud*.

She hit the ladder and climbed. The silence followed like water flooding up behind her. Her fingers slipped, nails splitting on the rusted rungs. Somewhere below, she could *feel* their pursuit—not footsteps, but ripples of stillness racing upward.

She reached the hatch, slammed her shoulder into it. The latch refused.

Her pendant flared hot, brighter than she'd ever felt. She pressed it to the seal—once, twice—and it gave with a metallic gasp.

Air rushed in, wild and chaotic and *loud*. The sound of the world—cars, insects, waves—crashed over her like salvation.

She staggered out into the mangroves, gulping noise like oxygen. Behind her, the hatch hissed shut, sealing the dark away.

For several seconds, she could only kneel there, hands in the dirt, shaking. Then the realization hit her fully, cutting through the adrenaline.

The House of Silence wasn't feeding anymore. They were *purging*.

And their leader—whatever that translucent creature was—had no intention of coexisting.

They meant to starve the world of sound until nothing but them remained.

She wiped the grime from her face, the hum in her chest still trembling like a warning bell. The Maestra's words echoed back: *If you lose control, I'll end it myself.*

But this wasn't her losing control.

This was war.

And if the Prime Note had chosen her, it was time to find out why.

# XI

The city glowed like a fever that couldn't break.

By the time Nyla reached Midnight Tempo again, the clouds had thickened into the kind of bruised gray that promised rain but never delivered it. The whole skyline pulsed with artificial light—billboards flickering, car horns echoing wrong, the street sounds bending just slightly out of tune. She could *feel* the Prime Note under it all now, whispering beneath every streetlamp hum and half-broken traffic signal.

Her car rolled to a stop in the alley behind the club. Even before she stepped out, her skin prickled—the air tasted charged, metallic, sharp like ozone before a lightning strike. Something was off.

The club should've been asleep at this hour—crew gone home, lights dimmed, the main room quiet except for the deep mechanical breaths of the cooling system. Instead, the moment she keyed the back door open, her senses caught the rhythm of *others*.

Powerful ones.

The low hum of House frequency hit her chest like pressure from inside her ribs. Every vampire vibrated with a pitch unique to their lineage; right now, the club sang with at least a dozen, weaving through the walls like threads of tension.

Nyla stepped into the narrow service corridor, boots whispering against the tile, and paused by the corner where the hall opened into the main floor. The sound there wasn't music—it was too precise, too contained. Resonance control training. Enforcers.

Her stomach tightened.

She moved carefully, following the vibrations up through the hall until the lights changed from red standby to the sterile white glow reserved for Council proceedings.

And there they were.

Studio A—the heart of Arista, her booth, her sanctuary—looked transformed into a tribunal. Ardelia stood at the center, her robe uncharacteristically plain, her hair pulled back in the severe braid she reserved for political bloodletting. Around her, three Council enforcers in white-and-silver armor waited in perfect stillness. The emblem of the unified Houses—three interlocked spirals—glimmered faintly on their chests.

Marisol stood near the back, arms folded, expression tight. Kian was beside her, hands bound with glimmerwire—a restraint that didn't cut flesh but trapped resonance. The strands pulsed faintly, matching the rhythm of his heartbeat. He looked calm, but his silence was heavier than usual—defensive, not natural.

When Ardelia's eyes lifted to meet Nyla's, something in the room shifted.

"Close the door," the Maestra said. Her voice was soft, but it left no room for argument.

Nyla obeyed, jaw tight. "What's going on?"

Ardelia's gaze flicked toward Kian, then back to her. "You tell me."

Nyla's pulse jumped. "You're going to have to be more specific."

"Don't mock me, Nyla." Ardelia's tone held the kind of calm that came right before storms. "The Council has learned of your connection to a registered hybrid of the House of Silence. You've withheld that information during an active investigation."

Nyla blinked, then glanced toward Kian. "You told them?"

He didn't answer.

She felt her throat tighten, a low vibration crawling up the back of her neck. "No. No, that's not. He wouldn't."

Ardelia cut in sharply. "He didn't need to. They already knew. His birth was recorded decades ago, though the files were sealed under treaty. He's been living under an alias."

Kian's jaw clenched. "I came here to stop the collapses, not cause them."

"And yet they follow you," said one of the enforcers. His voice was mechanical, filtered through the resonance suppressor built into his mask. "Silence walks in your wake."

"That's not how it works," Kian said evenly. "If it were, we'd all be gone already."

Ardelia lifted a hand, silencing the enforcer. Her focus stayed on Nyla. "Tell me the truth. Did you know what he was?"

Nyla hesitated.

The silence stretched too long.

"Answer me," Ardelia said.

"I knew," Nyla said finally. "But not at first. Not until—"

"Until you let him into your resonance field."

It wasn't phrased like a question. It was an indictment.

Nyla's cheeks flushed, but she held her ground. "I let him in because he helped me survive the rooftop collapse. Without him, half the pier would've been erased."

"And without him," said the enforcer, "the Prime Note would never have awakened at all."

The words landed like a punch.

Nyla looked between them, disbelief turning to anger. "You think *I* caused this because I fed from him? That's absurd."

"Absurd or not," Ardelia said, "it's evidence."

"Evidence of what? That I'm alive? That I did what I had to do to protect this House while you sat in meetings?"

Ardelia's face flickered—pain? Pride? It was impossible to tell. "You don't understand what you've unleashed."

Nyla stepped forward, the floor vibrating faintly with her resonance. "Then *tell me.* Stop speaking in riddles and codes. Tell me what the Prime Note really is."

Ardelia's composure cracked for half a second. "It's extinction," she whispered.

The word hung heavy in the air.

Nyla stared at her. "You've known this entire time, haven't you? The Prime Note isn't power—it's a weapon."

"The first and last sound," Ardelia said quietly. "It ends what it touches. When it sang in the old world, whole Houses fell silent. We buried it so deeply we thought we'd lost it forever. But it doesn't disappear—it waits."

"And now it's waiting for me."

Ardelia didn't answer.

Kian's voice broke through the tension. "She didn't summon it on purpose. It responded to her because her bloodline's tuned to its frequency."

"You're saying she's a conductor," one of the enforcers said.

"I'm saying she's *the* conductor," Kian replied. "The Prime Note won't rest until she finishes what it started."

"Then she must be contained," said the enforcer, stepping forward. "And the hybrid detained for interrogation."

Nyla moved fast. "You're not taking him."

Two enforcers flanked her immediately, their resonance fields buzzing like static barriers. She could feel the suppression wave clawing at her senses, thinning the air around her.

"Stand down," Ardelia said, voice low. "She's still under my jurisdiction."

"For now," the enforcer said.

Ardelia's gaze didn't waver. "You forget yourself."

He hesitated, bowing his head slightly. "Our orders are clear, Maestra. The Council wants the hybrid contained at Headquarters by dawn."

Kian's voice was calm but sharp. "If you think interrogating me will stop the collapses, you're already too late."

"Then perhaps we'll start with pain," the enforcer said.

The hum that followed wasn't loud, but the pressure made Nyla's vision blur. She moved before thinking, grabbing the nearest resonance conduit—the steel mic stand leaning against the console—and slammed it down, releasing a burst of pure frequency. The enforcer staggered back, armor flaring white.

"Enough!" Ardelia's voice cracked through the chaos like lightning. Every sound in the room obeyed her command; even the echoes froze.

The stillness after was suffocating.

Ardelia turned to Nyla. "You've already cost me the Council's trust. Don't cost me their mercy."

Nyla's throat burned. "Mercy? You're letting them take him!"

"I'm keeping you alive," Ardelia said. "If they see you defend a hybrid, they'll label you compromised."

"I *am* compromised," Nyla said. "That's what happens when you start seeing the enemy as human."

For the first time, Ardelia's expression softened, almost maternal. "Then you've learned the oldest mistake of our kind."

The enforcers seized Kian. He didn't resist, though his silence vibrated with something dangerous beneath it.

As they dragged him toward the exit, he caught Nyla's gaze. "Don't let them turn you into their weapon."

And then he was gone.

The door closed, leaving only the fading hum of the restraints and the heavy ache in Nyla's chest.

Ardelia exhaled slowly. "The Council will put you under watch until the situation stabilizes."

"House arrest," Nyla said bitterly.

"Containment," Ardelia corrected. "They'll monitor your resonance output. If it spikes, they'll send a warden. You'll have food, space, safety. Use the time to remember who you serve."

"I remember," Nyla said. "I just don't believe it anymore."

Marisol stepped forward then, worry written across her face. "Nyla—"

But Nyla was already walking away. "Don't. You picked your side the moment you stayed quiet."

She didn't look back as the doors sealed behind her.

The echo of them closing followed her down the corridor—a slow metallic inhale that seemed to stretch long after the sound should have faded. Every step she took felt heavier, the floor beneath her pulsing with the faint vibration of the House's infrastructure—a living thing thrumming beneath her boots, aware of her guilt even if she wasn't ready to name it.

Two enforcers flanked her in silence. No one spoke. No one had to. The air was dense enough to carry its own judgment.

They led her through a part of the building she'd never seen before, past rehearsal halls and mixing bays long abandoned. The deeper they went, the colder it became, the scent of ozone giving way to metal and damp stone. The hum that usually filled every inch of the House of Sound was gone here. Instead, there was a hollow quiet, the kind that left her pulse feeling like an intrusion.

Nyla kept her chin up, though her insides burned. Every hallway felt narrower than the last. Resonance-dampeners lined the walls, sleek black disks that throbbed faintly with blue light. They drained the air of vibration, flattening it until even her breathing sounded mechanical.

At one point, she thought she heard a faint echo behind one of the closed studio doors—a soft, rhythmic tap. Then nothing. It wasn't unusual for Resonants under sanction to be kept in isolation for recalibration. But it was the first time she realized just how many doors this place had. How many secrets were hidden behind them.

Her guards stopped at a seamless stretch of wall. One of them pressed a palm against the sensor plate. A quiet beep. Then the wall split open, revealing a narrow glass passageway that led down into the sublevel she didn't know existed.

As they walked, the glow of the House above grew dim, swallowed by the sterile white light below. The air turned clinical—no trace of music, no trace of warmth. Just that faint chemical scent that clung to hospitals and laboratories, places where sound went to die.

"What is this?" she asked, voice low.

Neither guard answered. One gestured her forward.

The corridor ended in a circular antechamber. The walls were paneled with mirrored glass, reflecting her face back a dozen times, fractured, disoriented. In the center was a single door with no handle, no lock—only a faint hum beneath the surface, one she recognized instinctively. A containment field.

The taller guard finally spoke. "Maestra's orders. Temporary residence."

"Residence?" Nyla laughed once, sharp and hollow. "You mean confinement."

Neither reacted. The field shimmered, parting just wide enough for her to step through.

The moment she crossed the threshold, the air changed. It was subtle—like stepping into a vacuum. Every sound she carried with her vanished, swallowed whole. Her boots hit the floor in silence. Her breath made no noise. Even her heartbeat dulled to a vibration she could feel but not hear.

The door sealed behind her, cutting the world away.

She stood there for a long moment, staring at the walls, her reflection warping in the faint metal sheen.

Her pendant glowed faintly against her skin, the only thing that still pulsed with life. She touched it, feeling the faint tremor of her own frequency struggling against the suppressors hidden in the walls. For the first time in a long time, she was truly alone—with nothing but the memory of what she'd done and the echo of what she'd lost.

She exhaled, and the air didn't answer back.

The isolation suite wasn't a cell, but it may as well have been. The walls were padded with resonance-dampening panels that absorbed every trace of her hum. The air smelled faintly of copper and disinfectant, the metallic scent of containment. There was no window, just a digital viewport projecting a looping image of the bay at night—silent waves, unmoving stars.

When she spoke, her voice came back dull, flat, stripped of warmth. She could feel the suppressor collar hidden in the room's architecture—a soft magnetic ring keeping her frequency two octaves below normal. It made her skin crawl.

She paced. The air vibrated faintly underfoot, but she couldn't push it. Her resonance had nowhere to go.

On the third hour, the comm-link on the wall flickered. Ardelia's face appeared, translucent.

"You're not my prisoner," she said.

"You could've fooled me."

"I'm trying to keep you alive long enough to understand what's coming."

"Then talk," Nyla said. "Tell me why Kian's bloodline scares you so much."

Ardelia hesitated. "The hybrids were designed for one purpose—to erase. The House of Silence created them to neutralize resonance. They're the perfect balance of flesh and void."

"And yet you let one work beside me."

"I didn't know who he was until tonight."

Nyla laughed once, bitter. "You always know. You just pretend it's strategy when it's convenience."

Ardelia's expression flickered, but she didn't argue. "If they extract what's in him, they'll find the same signal that woke in you. Then they'll use it."

"And when they do?"

"Then none of us will have a House left to fight for."

The feed went dead.

The wall screen dimmed to black, its faint hum collapsing into absolute stillness. For a moment, Nyla just stared at her reflection in the glass — her own face ghosted over the dark, the red glow of her pendant pulsing in her throat like a slow warning light. Then that, too, faded. The silence reasserted itself, heavy and complete.

She waited for the system to blink back to life. For Ardelia's voice to return, sharp and calm and endlessly composed. It didn't.

The stillness pressed closer. It was a silence designed to correct behavior, to smooth sharp edges. A kind of sonic punishment that worked better than pain ever could. Every second without sound stretched longer, scraping against her sense of self until she couldn't tell where her thoughts ended and the quiet began.

She tried to speak — just to hear a voice, even if it was her own — but the room swallowed her words. Her mouth moved, her throat worked, but the air refused to carry the vibration. It was like shouting into a dream.

Panic fluttered under her ribs. She pressed both palms to the wall, trying to feel the faintest trace of hum through the dampening panels. Nothing. No resonance. No heartbeat beyond her own.

They hadn't just locked her in. They'd tuned her *out.*

Nyla paced. Back and forth, back and forth, her steps noiseless on the padded floor. Each time she passed the viewport, she caught the loop of the digital bay — a night sky that never shifted, waves that never broke. The simulation had no sound, no wind, no movement, just an image frozen at the moment before dawn. She began to count the pixels.

At first, she told herself it was only for a few hours. Long enough for Ardelia to negotiate, long enough for the Council to reconsider, long enough for someone to remember that she'd saved more lives than she'd endangered. But as the false night refused to end, the thought started to fray.

The hunger came next. Not for blood — she hadn't fed that way in years — but for resonance. For the subtle background hum of the world that proved she was still tethered to it. Without it, her body felt off-balance, her thoughts thinning at the edges. Her power needed friction, something to vibrate against. Without it, she was static.

She tried to focus on memory instead. The taste of music under her skin. The smell of the club after hours — bass and perfume and dust. The feel of Kian's hand steadying her when everything else was shaking. She clung to those details like talismans, afraid that if she forgot them, the silence would claim the rest.

At some point, she lost count of how many times she'd slept, or if she even had. The artificial light above her dimmed and brightened in an unsteady rhythm, simulating day cycles that meant nothing down here.

Once, she thought she heard something — a faint thud, maybe footsteps in the hall. She pressed her ear to the wall, desperate for proof she wasn't the only thing left alive in this frequencyless world.

Nothing.

But then, faintly, she *felt* something instead.

Not sound — more like memory of sound. A vibration through the floor, too subtle for human detection but impossible for a Resonant to ignore. A rhythm like breath, slow and patient.

It wasn't the guards. It wasn't Ardelia.

It was the city.

Even here, beneath layers of suppression, she could feel it — the Prime Note's pulse threading its way through concrete and circuitry, brushing the edge of her awareness like fingertips tracing glass.

She closed her eyes, fighting the pull. The silence didn't want to keep her safe. It wanted to make her listen.

And as she stood there, palms flat against the wall, she realized what terrified her most.

She wasn't sure she could tell the difference anymore — between the silence the Council built to contain her, and the one that had come looking for her from beneath the bay.

Days passed — or maybe hours. In the soundproofed room, time was another frequency, warped and endless. Occasionally, she heard footsteps outside her door — guards rotating shifts, whispering to each other about containment risk.

But it wasn't the guards that worried her. It was the cracks.

Not in the walls. In *them.*

Whispers rippled through the House of Sound like feedback through a faulty wire. She could feel it through the concrete—Resonants turning on each other, accusing, afraid. Some believed she was the Prime's chosen conductor. Others thought she was the beginning of the end.

And Ardelia... she was losing them.

From her cell, Nyla could sense it—the Maestra's frequency, once pure and commanding, now fractured into competing rhythms. Council oversight. Internal rebellion. Fear spreading like smoke.

The House of Sound had always thrived on harmony. But harmony required trust, and trust had turned brittle.

Now, when she pressed her palm to the wall, she didn't feel the familiar pulse of unity she'd grown up in.

She felt noise.

Wild, discordant, human noise.

The House was unraveling.

And in the distance, under the waves of static that were quickly becoming the soundtrack of her confinement, the hum of the Prime Note grew louder—patient, inevitable, and far too close to home.

# XII: KIAN

They cuffed my resonance before they cuffed my wrists.

Standard protocol for hybrids. Can't risk a half-blood nulling a frequency lock. Glimmerwire—thin as spider silk, bright as sin—wound tight around my forearms, humming softly in tune with my pulse. It didn't hurt. Not physically. But the silence that followed did.

The sound of your own heartbeat, when it's all you have left, starts to feel like mockery.

They walked me through the main hall of the House of Sound like I was a contagion. Eyes followed. Resonants I'd trained beside, fought beside, pretended to belong among. Now their frequencies recoiled instinctively as I passed, their hums flattening into defensive static. It wasn't fear—they didn't fear me. It was worse than that. It was disgust.

House of Silence, they whispered. Hybrid. Damper. Traitor.

I didn't correct them. They were all right.

The enforcers kept pace at my sides—two white-armored ghosts with their resonance fields tuned to cancel out mine. It was effective. Every time I tried to reach into the air, to feel the music of the world around me, it slipped away like oil on water. My silence against their silence. I'd forgotten how lonely it was when you couldn't feel the hum.

They led me down a flight of concrete stairs, through a hall so sterile I could smell the disinfectant through my teeth. The door at the end opened with a hiss.

Council holding cell. Neutral ground. Nowhere, basically.

The room was small—metal walls, no windows, a single light that never flickered. Resonance-dampening technology embedded everywhere, from the floor grates to the air filters. The kind of silence engineered, not born.

They pushed me inside. The door sealed behind me with a pneumatic sigh.

I exhaled slowly, sinking onto the cold bench attached to the wall. My wrists buzzed with residual static. I turned them slightly, watching the glimmerwire react—brightening, then dimming, a heartbeat of containment. I could break it if I really wanted to. Every hybrid could, though few ever lived to tell anyone afterward. The last Damper who tried left a crater where his head used to be.

So, no. Not tonight.

I sat there instead, letting my mind drift. It was easier than thinking.

I've never liked the word "hybrid." It sounds clean. Scientific. It isn't. It's messy, accidental. A reminder that the Houses aren't as separate as they pretend.

My mother was human. A field researcher in Havana when the 1962 collapse hit. She was studying seismic patterns when the city started to sing. The resonance quake. She survived. Most didn't. The ones who did were changed—frequencies warped, senses rewired. My father found her a week later, half-conscious in a hospital that couldn't stop vibrating. He was House of Silence. Sent to neutralize her before the infection spread.

He didn't.

I was the result.

Silence doesn't fall in love. That's what they tell you. They don't make music, they erase it. They call it balance. Detachment. The absence of chaos. But every void craves something to fill it.

That's where I come from.

When I was old enough to stand on my own resonance, the Council found me. "Asset" was the word they used. A bridge between frequencies. An experiment that didn't end in disaster. I was raised half by scientists, half by soldiers, trained to neutralize resonance in combat zones, rogue Houses, riots.

I learned early that I wasn't supposed to feel anything about it. Silence isn't moral. It's mathematical. But somewhere along the way, I started to envy the ones I was sent to suppress. The ones who *felt* their power. Who could sing the world into motion.

Maybe that's why I joined the House of Sound.

They told me to infiltrate, to observe. But I didn't infiltrate anything. I walked in, tuned to their key, and they never even noticed. I learned to fake the hum. For a while, I even believed it.

Then Nyla happened.

She wasn't the first Resonant I'd met, but she was the first who didn't flinch at the silence that followed me. She leaned into it. She said it made her music sharper. I thought she was joking.
She wasn't.

When she played, I could *feel* again. Not just the sound—everything. The space between the notes, the air changing color around her, the rhythm that existed before language. She had no idea what she was doing. The Prime Note wasn't supposed to wake, but she carried it like it had been waiting for her blood all along.

The Council thinks she's dangerous. They're wrong. She's worse than that. She's inevitable.

I run my hands over my face, dragging away the residue of too many thoughts. The cell hums faintly now—a containment frequency adjusting to my stress levels. My silence pushes against it instinctively, flattening the pitch, making it wobble.

It's almost a game. Almost.

The door hisses open.

An enforcer steps in first, followed by a woman I've seen before. Council liaison. No House affiliation visible. Her resonance is faint—controlled to the point of invisibility.
She sets a tablet on the metal table between us. "Kian Redd."

"That's me."

"Hybrid of Silence and mortal lineage. Registered under false sponsorship within the House of Sound for seven years."

"Eight."

She doesn't smile. "You've been embedded long enough to report on every significant Resonant within that House. Yet, the Council notes several inconsistencies in your documentation. You've omitted one name repeatedly."

I meet her eyes. "Let me guess."

"Nyla Voss."

Her tone gives nothing away, but I can feel the shift in the room's vibration—subtle, calculated. She's watching my pulse through the wire.

"She's irrelevant," I say.

"She awakened the Prime Note."

"I didn't teach her that."

"But you fed her."

"That's not a crime."

"In this context, it is."

I lean back, biting back a laugh. "The Council's finally running out of villains, huh? So now it's lovers on the list?"

"You misunderstand," she says. "This isn't punishment. It's precaution."

"Precaution against what?"

She folds her hands. "You. The last hybrid who carried Prime resonance destroyed an entire city. You want us to risk that again?"

I stare at her. "You really think that's what she is? A bomb waiting to sing herself to death?"

"I think she's a weapon without a conductor."

"She's a person."

"A person who doesn't know what she's become," the woman says. "And you—you're the tether. The null point. If she unravels, you could stop her."

I exhale slowly. "You don't want me to stop her. You want me to pull the trigger."

Silence.
That's my answer.

When they leave, they take the light with them. The cell dims, settling into that familiar dark hum I grew up with—the lullaby of my father's kind.

I let my mind wander back to Nyla. The way she moved when she played. The way her voice changed the air. She's too much for this world—too bright, too loud, too alive. The Council will never understand that kind of beauty. They'll cage it, smother it, or bury it beneath their treaties.

But she doesn't belong to them. Not anymore.

After they left me alone in the cell, I waited for the silence to settle, for it to become the kind I could control—the kind I'd been born to weaponize. But this wasn't my silence. This was theirs. Synthetic. Sterile. Engineered to hum at just the right frequency to make me feel small inside it.

That's how the Council disciplines half-breeds: they drown you in imitation quiet, until you start forgetting what true stillness sounds like.

I sat there with my wrists still bound, the glimmerwire pulsing faintly every few seconds like a reminder of my bloodline—half human, half monster, wholly inconvenient. The ache under my skin wasn't pain. It was the constant, low-grade pressure of being contained. A Damper's curse: we feel silence like other people feel gravity. It's always pressing down.

I should have been angry, but I wasn't. Anger takes energy. Silence feeds on it. The more you fight, the more it wins. So I breathed slow, counting the seconds in heartbeats, waiting for something—anything—to break.

They didn't even bother to interrogate me again. Not yet. The Council liked to marinate you first, to let the quiet strip away everything that made you resist. It was how they trained Dampers: isolation until surrender felt like peace. I'd spent years in rooms like this.

But not since Nyla.

Thinking her name felt like a sin. The room seemed to darken around it.

Nyla Voss. I tried not to imagine what they were doing to her—what Ardelia was doing to her. The Council would never kill her outright, not while the Prime Note still pulsed in her veins. They'd cage her in soundproof velvet, study her like an instrument. And when they learned how she worked, they'd strip her of it. They always did.

I leaned back against the wall, letting my head fall back until it hit metal. The sound that didn't come hurt worse than a blow. My mind went to her again—her voice, her laugh, that impossible energy she carried like the world itself was a stage she refused to dim for.

She'd looked at me like I wasn't something to fix. Like the silence in me wasn't a void, but a home she could walk into and leave music behind.

And now she was alone.

I wanted to believe Ardelia would protect her, but I'd seen the look in the Maestra's eyes during the tribunal—conflict disguised as control. She wouldn't save Nyla. She'd preserve the House.

That's the thing about the Houses—they pretend to be families, but they're really just factions with better branding.

House of Sound, House of Silence, House of Smoke, House of Stone. Each convinced they're protecting balance, when really they're protecting ego.

Silence pretends to keep order, Sound pretends to celebrate freedom, Smoke sells illusions, and Stone buries truth. But they're all just remnants of what we used to be:

one fractured frequency, pretending the split made us stronger.

The Council loves that myth. They call it evolution. I call it entropy with better PR.

I tried to focus on the present, but my thoughts kept drifting back to her—to the way her resonance felt when it collided with mine. The moment we fed, something in me shifted. I'd spent my whole life trained to erase sound, to nullify vibration before it reached chaos. But she wasn't chaos. She was clarity disguised as noise.

I'd told myself I could handle it—that I could stay detached. But the second her hum touched mine, I knew I'd been lying for years. Silence isn't the absence of feeling; it's the accumulation of too much of it. And she cracked it open with a single breath.

I should have stayed away. Should have finished the mission, handed my report to the Council, and disappeared like the good half-breed they thought I was. But when she looked at me, I remembered what it felt like to be *heard*.

And now I was paying for it.

The containment field hummed faintly against my skin. I could almost see the vibration in the air—a transparent shimmer, delicate but absolute. Beyond it, faint light spilled from the corridor, reflecting on the polished steel walls. The smell of ozone lingered, the byproduct of constant resonance suppression. The kind of air that made breathing feel optional.

They'd come back for me eventually. Ask me questions in polite tones. Maybe they'd offer me freedom in exchange for betrayal. They always did. But I'd already made my choice.

I shifted my hands, testing the wire. It bit into my wrists—not sharp, but cold, numbing. It was designed to tune itself to the subject's internal frequency. The harder you pulled, the tighter it bound. Most vampires screamed when it hit bone. I didn't. Pain's just another kind of vibration, and I'd spent a lifetime learning how to hold it until it dissolved.

Somewhere far above me, the building trembled—barely perceptible, but there. A faint reverberation through the foundation, like thunder buried in the walls. A resonance surge, maybe. Or a House collapsing.

I closed my eyes, reaching for the sound even though I knew I shouldn't. The dampeners dulled it, but not completely. There it was again—the faintest echo, bleeding through the silence. Nyla's hum.

I didn't hear it with my ears. I felt it in my bones.

She was still alive, and that changed everything.

The fear that had sat coiled behind my ribs uncurled into something else—resolve. If she was alive, the Note was still singing. If the Note was still singing, it wasn't done with either of us.

I straightened, hands steady, breath measured. The Council thought they understood silence, thought they could own it. They'd forgotten that silence isn't control—it's resistance.

I smiled then, small and quiet.

Let them come.

Let them talk about containment, about duty, about the cost of imbalance.

Let them think I'm still theirs.

Because Nyla doesn't belong to them, and neither do I.

Hours pass. Or days. Hard to tell when you're living in a clock with no sound. The human part of me itches for rhythm, for measure. Silence isn't absence—it's suspension. Every second hangs midair until it decides to die.

I close my eyes and start to hum—not out loud, but inside. A vibration no one else can hear. A trick I learned in training: internal resonance. The body as instrument, the bones as tuning fork. It steadies the mind.

Through the silence, I can almost feel her. Nyla's hum is distinct—warm, sharp-edged, threaded with defiance. The kind of tone you could build a religion around. It's faint now, like she's behind glass. But she's there.

I imagine her pacing a small room somewhere in the sublevels. I imagine her eyes burning holes through the walls. I imagine the hum under her skin growing restless, the Prime Note shifting every time she breathes.

If I concentrate hard enough, I can feel it through the concrete—a pulse buried in the earth beneath Miami. The Note itself, waiting.

They call it the first sound. The echo that separated creation from chaos. But the truth is uglier. The Prime Note isn't divine. It's entropy. It doesn't sing; it devours. It equalizes everything to silence. The Houses were built to keep that from happening again—to maintain the illusion of balance.

Silence. Sound. Smoke. Stone. Four fragments of a broken scale, pretending they could exist apart. Each convinced their pitch was the pure one. They forget that purity is what killed the first world.

I know what the Council's really afraid of. Not Nyla. Not me. The *merge.*

If a Resonant of Sound and a Damper of Silence align perfectly, they don't cancel each other. They complete the scale. The Prime Note returns. Balance, yes—but not the kind anyone survives.

That's what my father used to say when he thought I was asleep. *You can't build peace from halves, Kian. You just make new wars that sound prettier.*

Maybe he was right.

My father always said there were two kinds of peace: the kind you build and the kind that buries you. He'd learned the difference the hard way—kneeling in front of the Council with his resonance stripped from his throat, branded a traitor for refusing to nullify a city full of his own. I used to think he was a coward for letting them take everything from him. Now, sitting in this cell, I understood. Some silences weren't made to be fought. They were made to be endured.

The air in here carried that same sterile quiet—the kind that didn't just mute sound, it hollowed it. The hum of the containment field blended with my pulse until I couldn't tell where I ended and the technology began. They'd built this chamber like a monastery for punishment, not prayer.

I leaned my head back against the wall, eyes closed. The ceiling vibrated faintly, the residue of activity far above. I could sense it through the layers of dampening material—Resonants moving, arguing, feeding the walls their tension. Even silence had seams if you knew how to listen.

I tried to reach for the frequency that was Nyla's—warm, sharp-edged, impossible to contain. It wasn't there. Or maybe I couldn't feel it from here. That terrified me more than the idea of dying.

For a long time, I just sat and breathed. Counted the beats between heart and hum. A Damper's meditation. Inhale. Exhale. Let the body tune itself to the room. Find the lowest frequency and disappear into it.

It worked. Sort of. The noise in my head quieted. The ache in my ribs softened. For a few minutes, I wasn't a prisoner. I was a part of the system—one more piece of engineered silence holding the House together.

But I couldn't hold it forever.

The longer I stayed still, the more the silence began to crawl. That's what people never understand about my kind—true silence is never calm. It's alive. It watches. It waits for you to slip, to fill it with something it can devour. The walls seemed to breathe around me, metal expanding and contracting with faint, rhythmic patience.

I could feel my thoughts start to drift—back to Havana, to the training compounds, to the first time they'd made me neutralize a Resonant. A woman barely older than Nyla, trembling with sound that wouldn't stop spilling out of her. They called it an accident. I called it murder. When the quiet finally took her, I'd felt it inside me like a shudder. A connection I never wanted but couldn't erase.

That's when I stopped believing in Houses. Stopped believing in "balance." We were never balance. We were just different brands of control.

The lights above flickered once, a soft pulse through the glass. Maybe power fluctuation. Maybe the city outside shaking again. The Prime Note, restless beneath it all.

I rubbed my wrists against the glimmerwire, more out of habit than defiance. The strands warmed slightly, reading the shift in my blood. They wanted me calm. Contained. Predictable.

Instead, I started humming.

It was barely audible, a note too low for human ears, but it was mine—the same pitch I used to keep my resonance steady when missions went sideways. The Council hated when Dampers hummed. Said it blurred the line between containment and creation. They weren't wrong.

I felt the hum bounce back at me from the walls, altered. The dampeners caught it, reshaped it, sent it looping in on itself. Within seconds the air felt charged, alive, like standing in the center of a thunderhead.

Good. Let them hear me. Let them remember that even Silence makes noise when it wants to.

The door lock clicked. Once. Twice. The hum died instantly, swallowed by the containment field reasserting itself.

I straightened, hands on my knees, pulse steady.

The air outside shifted—movement, the scent of static and ozone. Not a guard. Too careful for that. Too *present.*

The door opens again sometime later—no knock, no warning. Just a rush of air, a shadow, and then Ardelia herself steps through.

She looks smaller without the Council robe. Tired, but still impossible to ignore. Her resonance is muted, but I can feel it—the weight of leadership, of centuries.

"I told them not to hurt her," she says.

I don't look up. "And they listened?"

"They're still listening now. Every word we say is monitored."

"Then let's make it interesting."

She sighs, crossing the small space to stand opposite me. "I didn't know who you were. If I had—"

"You'd have killed me?"

"Maybe."

I almost smile. "You'd have had to get in line."

She studies me for a long time, her gaze sharp but not cruel. "You care for her."

"I do."

"Then you'll understand what I'm asking."

"Let me guess—help you keep her alive long enough to sacrifice her later?"

Ardelia's jaw tightens. "You think I want this?"

"I think you'll do it anyway."

She doesn't deny it. "If the Prime Note consumes her, she'll take the rest of us with her. I can't let that happen."

"She's not a monster."

"She's becoming something older than monsters."

I stand then, the glimmerwire catching the dim light between us. "You talk about her like she's some legend you're trying to rewrite. But she's flesh and breath and choice. You taught her that. You taught her to listen."

Ardelia's eyes flicker—pain, pride, grief all tangled. "And I taught her what happens when we don't."

She turns to leave, then pauses. "When they transfer you to Council custody, they'll ask you to neutralize her. Don't let them make you believe it's mercy."

And then she's gone.

The door whispered shut behind her, sealing the air with that soft, hydraulic finality the Council seemed to favor. It wasn't a slam, wasn't a click—just the kind of sound designed to erase itself the moment it existed. Like she'd never been there at all.

I sat there, staring at the space she'd left behind. The scent of her—amber and static and something faintly metallic—still lingered in the room, mingling with the cold tang of glimmerwire. I let it sit on my tongue a moment longer than I should have, trying to decide what I felt.

Not anger. Not exactly. Ardelia had never lied to me. She didn't have to. She told the truth like a blade—efficient, practiced, cutting only as deep as necessary.

But she'd still cut.

I could still hear the echo of her words in the back of my skull: *Don't let them make you believe it's mercy.*

Mercy. That was rich, coming from the Council's finest weapon. The Houses had a funny way of dressing up cruelty in softer words. Containment became protection. Assassination became cleansing. Mercy was just what they called silence when it suited them.

I leaned back against the wall, closing my eyes. My wrists ached from the restraints, but the ache felt grounding. Real. The rest of it—Ardelia's visit, her half-threat, half-confession—it all felt like a fever dream.

She wanted me to help her keep Nyla alive. The same Nyla she'd locked away. The same Nyla the Council now wanted to dissect. I didn't know whether to laugh or scream.

Instead, I breathed.

For a long time, the cell stayed dim and still. The light above me flickered once—barely noticeable—but it was enough. The silence rippled. Silence always *ripples,* if you pay attention. It's never as pure as they pretend. It's layers of waiting sound, air pressure, unspoken thought.

And I started thinking about her again..

She'd said once that silence scared her. Not because it was empty, but because it *listened.* She wasn't wrong. It always listened. I wondered if, right now, she could feel it pressing against her walls the way I could. I wondered if she knew that somewhere, beneath all the containment and circuitry, we were still connected—two frequencies circling each other through the static.

That connection wasn't supposed to exist. Sound and silence weren't meant to harmonize. But when she'd touched me, when her resonance had tangled with mine, something ancient in both of us had recognized the truth the Houses kept buried: we were never enemies. We were halves of the same impossible song.

I opened my eyes again. The light had dimmed further. The air hummed faintly—low, constant. A pulse through the walls. I couldn't tell if it came from the dampeners or from me.

Ardelia had warned me that the Prime Note would consume her if left unchecked. But what she didn't say—what she couldn't say—was that it had already started consuming me.

The Note didn't just awaken in Nyla. It resonated through everything she touched. I'd seen it in the bay water, felt it under my skin, in the stillness of every room she left behind. The Prime Note wasn't music—it was contagion. And I'd been infected.

I rubbed my hands together, palms slick with sweat. My pulse thudded unevenly, too fast, too shallow. A Damper wasn't supposed to feel resonance. Not like this. My silence should've neutralized it. But the hum in my veins wouldn't stop. It was faint but persistent, like the memory of a melody you couldn't quite shake.

I tried to steady my breathing. It didn't help. Every inhale felt louder than the last, every exhale sharper. I could almost *see* it now—faint wisps of vibration trailing from my fingertips, bending the air in microscopic waves.

I thought about Ardelia again, her eyes when she said she'd kill Nyla if she had to. There had been a flicker there—fear, not conviction. And fear meant she didn't know everything either.

Good.

If the Maestra of Sound could be afraid, maybe that meant there was still a note left in the song none of them could hear yet.

The hum inside me built, then broke, collapsing into a softer rhythm that almost sounded like a heartbeat that wasn't mine.

It took me a moment to realize what it was.

Even locked away, even muted, I could still *feel* her—the faint resonance signature of her presence cutting through the dampeners like a single note piercing glass.

I let it wash over me, steady and painful. The Prime Note between us pulsed once, like recognition.

And then it stopped.

I was alone again.

But the silence didn't feel empty anymore. It felt... waiting. Charged. Listening.

After she leaves, the silence feels different. I let my hands fall to my lap, the glimmerwire cool against my skin. There's a faint tremor running through it now—not mechanical, not external. It's *response.* My resonance pushing back.

Something's happening above. I can feel it in the air—the static of panic, the discord of too many frequencies colliding. The House of Sound is fracturing.

I close my eyes and picture Nyla again, her voice cutting through the quiet like sunrise through fog. The world doesn't deserve her kind of noise. But I do.

If she burns, I burn too. That's the math of it. Silence and sound, wound together until neither remembers who started the song.

So when the glimmerwire finally gives beneath my skin, I don't hesitate.

The containment field flickers once, startled.

And for the first time in years, I let myself hum out loud—low and steady, the frequency of defiance.

Somewhere beyond the walls, I swear I hear her answer.

# XIII: NYLA

The storm had been sitting over the city for three days, smothering the skyline in gray. Thunder rolled through the distance like the earth was clearing its throat, but no rain ever came. The humidity hung thick and electric — a perfect conductor for secrets.

By the time Nyla escaped containment, the House of Sound no longer sounded like home. It *felt* different, too. The familiar vibration in the walls — the heartbeat of every Resonant's pulse syncing together — was fractured. Broken. The corridors still thrummed with activity, but the rhythm had changed. Fear had a pitch, and she could hear it everywhere.

Marisol met her at the back entrance of Studio B, hair pulled tight beneath a hood, eyes rimmed with sleeplessness. She didn't say anything, just handed Nyla her pendant — confiscated, muted, but still warm to the touch.

"You didn't get this from me," Marisol said.

Nyla clasped it around her neck. "You keep saying that, and I keep pretending to believe it."

"Then we're even."

Tavi arrived a few minutes later, breathless from the run, glitter worn dull from rain. "Just like old times," she said, glancing around. "Except the part where we're committing treason."

"Only if we get caught," Nyla said.

"Oh, we're definitely getting caught."

The three of them moved quickly through the service corridor, avoiding the main halls where Council enforcers patrolled. Their resonance signatures were disguised — a distortion Marisol had rigged through her wrist comms, forcing their frequencies to loop on themselves like sonic camouflage. It wouldn't hold long, but it didn't have to.

They weren't going far.

Just to the vault.

The vault wasn't a place most Resonants even knew existed. Officially, it didn't. Hidden beneath the House archives, it had been built centuries ago to hold what Ardelia called *legacy sound* — recordings too dangerous to destroy but too sacred to share. The earliest symphonies of their kind. The first experiments with resonance. And, if Marisol's intel was right, the truth about the Prime Note.

They reached the security gate — a massive bronze door etched with harmonic script. It wasn't guarded. It didn't need to be. The door itself was alive, vibrating faintly, waiting to recognize a familiar frequency.

Nyla pressed her palm against the center glyph. The metal was cool—almost kind.

"It's coded to her," Marisol whispered. "Only the Maestra can open it."

"Then we'll borrow her key."

Nyla focused, letting her pulse steady. Ardelia's resonance still lived somewhere inside her — faint traces absorbed during every performance, every moment of training, every reprimand whispered through gritted teeth. The connection wasn't just metaphorical. When two Resonants shared sound for long enough, their frequencies could intertwine.

She breathed deep, remembering Ardelia's tone — low, deliberate, commanding. The hum of authority. She shaped it on her tongue like a memory. The door shivered.

Marisol's eyes widened. "You're doing it."

The glyphs began to glow, lines of pale gold running outward from Nyla's hand. The entire vault seemed to hold its breath.

Then—*click*.

The seal released.

The air that escaped was ancient—dust, copper, and the faint sweetness of forgotten blood.

Inside, the vault wasn't a room. It was a cathedral.

Circular, descending, carved from obsidian and glass, it looked like someone had hollowed out the inside of a great speaker and filled it with ghosts. Thousands of reels lined the walls, stacked in shimmering spirals, each one labeled in a dead language of frequency marks. The ceiling was a perfect dome that caught the faintest sound and sent it spinning back like light.

"Okay," Tavi whispered, craning her neck. "On a scale of one to full-blown apocalypse, where are we right now?"

"About an eight," Nyla said softly. "Maybe nine if we find what I think we will."

They descended the stairs, each step echoing faintly — not because of the space, but because of the memories trapped in the air. Every frequency that had ever played here lingered, vibrating just beneath audibility.

Marisol's scanner blinked. "There."

At the far end stood a sealed chamber—smaller, older. The plaque above the door read:

**ACCESS RESTRICTED**

Nyla stared at the lettering, her stomach tightening.

Tavi looked between them. "Prime like... prime steak? Or prime like we-should-turn-around-before-we-die?"

"Prime like everything ends if it plays wrong," Nyla said.

The lock on this chamber wasn't a glyph. It was voice-activated, with frequency recognition.

Marisol bit her lip. "It needs Ardelia's pitch signature."

Nyla exhaled. "She built this vault before I was born. Every Maestra of Sound adds to it. It has her voice layered into the key. But..." She trailed off, thinking.

"But?"

"I've performed with her for years. Our harmonics overlap."

"Tell me you're not—"

But she was already standing in front of the door, closing her eyes.

She let the room fall away, her focus narrowing to a single vibration—Ardelia's tone, deep and velvet, the voice that had taught her to control chaos, to turn hunger into melody. She mirrored it — perfectly, painfully.

The vault answered.

The door opened.

Inside was no archive. No shelf. Just a console and a projection table surrounded by glass cylinders filled with flickering light. Resonance itself, suspended like captured flame. The hum inside the room was low, harmonic, nearly human.

Marisol stepped forward, scanning the console. "These are original recordings," she whispered. "Not copies. The first echoes ever made."

Nyla moved closer to the center table. A single file glowed on the display labeled:

**MAESTRA INITIATIVE**

She opened it.

The vault lights dimmed. A holographic waveform unfurled in the air—wide, pulsating, hypnotic. Beneath it, lines of translation scrolled in faint gold script.

Tavi read aloud, voice trembling: "*The Prime Note — origin of resonance. The sound that gave hunger to blood and will to silence. Sealed beneath the world by the founding Houses. Controlled activation requires conduit. Conduit requires conductor. Conductor requires sacrifice."*

The words sank like stones.

Nyla's throat went dry. "She knew."

Marisol scanned another file, frowning. "This isn't just theory. There's recent data here. Current resonance logs—pulled from *you*."

"What?"

Tavi leaned in. "Wait, those numbers... are those from your performances?"

Marisol nodded grimly. "Every set you've played for the last year. Frequency readings, amplitude spikes, blood resonance signatures. She's been recording your output."

"She's been siphoning me," Nyla whispered. "All this time."

Tavi's eyes darted to the holographic waveform still flickering above them. "To activate *this*?"

"Yes."

Marisol looked at the time stamp on the final entry. "The last scheduled playback is tomorrow night. The House gala."

The realization hit hard, settling in Nyla's chest like lead. The gala—the annual showcase, broadcast across every House, every city, every system. Millions would be watching. And Ardelia would play the Note through *her*.

"She's going to unleash it," Nyla said. "Live."

Marisol's expression hardened. "If she does, it'll rewrite everything. The Houses won't exist after that. Vampiric resonance—feeding, hierarchy, bloodlines—it'll all collapse."

Tavi swallowed. "And humans?"

"Humans won't even remember we were here," Nyla said softly.

The vault seemed to breathe around them, the walls vibrating faintly as though aware they had uncovered something forbidden.

Marisol turned to Nyla. "We can't stop her from above. Not once she starts the sequence. You'd have to cut the signal from the core."

"The core's under the gala stage," Nyla said. "That's not security—it's suicide."

Tavi gave her a small, crooked smile. "Good thing I'm immortal and terrible at following rules."

Nyla didn't laugh. She couldn't. The room's hum had shifted again, rising into a tone so high it scraped her bones. The resonance in the cylinders flickered violently, as if sensing their panic.

She reached out, placing a hand on one of them. The vibration thrummed up her arm, wild and hungry.

It whispered in her head—*Conductor found*.

Nyla jerked back. The light inside the cylinder dimmed.

Marisol's scanner buzzed, frantic. "That wasn't playback," she said. "It was *response.*"

The vault doors groaned behind them. The harmonic glyphs began to dim one by one.

Tavi looked around, panicked. "Uh, we're not alone, are we?"

"No," Nyla said, turning toward the exit, her voice low and steady. "We just woke the Note."

The vault's light changed immediately—pale gold collapsing into a suffocating red. The hum that had filled the air deepened, becoming a pulse that seemed to come from the walls themselves. Every frequency in the room turned hostile.

The reels along the curved wall began to spin on their own. Dust rose in trembling clouds. The air grew thick enough to breathe wrong.

Tavi froze. "Um. That doesn't sound like gratitude."

Marisol swore under her breath and yanked at the scanner strapped to her wrist. "The vault's harmonic field is destabilizing. We need to go—now."

Nyla was already moving, her boots slipping slightly on the smooth obsidian floor as the vibration intensified. The staircase ahead of them shuddered, metal whining under the pressure. The vault was trying to contain what they'd awakened.

She glanced back once. The cylinders they'd disturbed were glowing again, brighter this time—one by one, like eyes opening after centuries of sleep. The faint hum built into a layered chord, then fractured into dissonance.

It wasn't music. It was warning.

Marisol grabbed Tavi by the arm and shoved her toward the stairs. "Go!"

They ran.

The climb up the spiral felt endless. The air vibrated so violently it blurred their vision; every breath tasted like copper and ozone. Symbols along the walls flared and went dark, shorting out as if rejecting them.

Halfway up, Tavi stumbled. Nyla caught her before she hit the steps. "Keep moving!"

"Easy for you to say!" Tavi wheezed. "You're the one the murder-music *likes!*"

A loud crack split the air behind them. The vault door had begun to close, sealing them in.

"Faster!" Marisol shouted, her voice nearly lost to the rising pitch. The stairwell was filling with resonance feedback, waves of invisible pressure slamming into their bodies like the deep bass of an explosion that never released.

Nyla could feel the Note in her bones now—each thrum aligning with her heartbeat until she couldn't tell which belonged to her. It wasn't calling her anymore. It was *following.*

By the time they reached the final step, the light above the doorway flickered violently. Marisol hit the panel on the wall, but it stayed dark.

"It's locked us in!" she yelled.

Nyla pushed her aside and pressed her hand to the door. The metal was hot under her palm, humming with recognition. She closed her eyes, forcing her own frequency higher, matching the pitch of the vault. The feedback screamed in her skull, but she held steady.

The door flared white, then burst open with a deafening pop. A wave of energy rolled past them—heat and cold at once—snuffing out the light in the stairwell.

They stumbled into the corridor above, lungs burning. Behind them, the vault sealed itself with a deep, final *thunk,* leaving only silence in its wake.

Tavi leaned against the wall, gasping. "Please tell me that was just an automated alarm system and not, you know, the ghost of the world's first song trying to eat us."

Marisol checked her scanner, the display flickering with corrupted data. "Whatever it was, it just spiked the entire House's grid. We're talking seismic-level resonance. It's bleeding into every floor."

Nyla steadied herself, eyes still glowing faintly from the residual energy. The hum inside her hadn't stopped. If anything, it was louder now, as though the Note had crawled beneath her skin and made itself comfortable.

"We can't stay down here," she said. "If the system detects a breach, it'll lock the sublevels. We'll be trapped."

Marisol nodded and started forward. "Then we move before it decides we're part of the vault."

They ran.

The stairwells trembled beneath their feet as they ascended. Dust fell from the ceiling in soft gray plumes, coating their shoulders, their hair. Somewhere in the distance, faint alarms tried to start but sputtered out—cut off mid-blare by interference from the Note's awakening.

Nyla glanced over her shoulder once more. The lower hall glowed faintly red, pulsing like a heartbeat deep underground. Whatever they'd disturbed was awake now. Listening.

The hum followed them all the way up.

They didn't speak again until they were topside, running through the dim corridors of the House, the alarms still silent but the walls trembling with anticipation.

Nyla stopped at the stairwell, catching her breath, heart hammering out an erratic rhythm that no music could contain.

"The gala starts at sundown," Marisol said. "If she plays it, everything changes."

Nyla nodded, eyes hard. "Then we change it first."

The storm outside rumbled louder, lightning flashing across the bay in jagged white veins. The city held its breath, waiting for the downbeat.

And somewhere in the distance, beneath the noise of thunder and the hum of frightened Resonants, the Prime Note purred. Soft, patient, inevitable.

# XIV

The city glimmered under the weight of stormlight. Clouds hung heavy over the skyline, the bay below pulsing with reflections of white and crimson. The House of Sound's annual gala had always been a spectacle, but tonight it was something else entirely. The lights felt wrong. Too precise. Every beam timed to an invisible rhythm that Nyla could feel thrumming through her chest.

She hadn't worn a disguise like this since the early years, when she'd still played human clubs for the thrill of danger. A low-slung black gown, hair slicked back to hide the shimmer in her veins, the faintest dusting of silver across her collarbones. On the surface, she looked like any performer hired to set the tone for the night. But the pendant at her throat still hummed softly, faint and alive, feeding her the pulse of the building itself.

The main hall of Arista House Records had been transformed into a cathedral of light. Glass walls reflected the rain outside, and the ceiling shimmered with suspended speakers arranged in concentric circles. The air vibrated with hundreds of Resonants, their laughter pitched like instruments tuning before a concert. A string quartet played something elegant and too slow, their music sterilized to the point of discomfort. The scent of ozone and iron lingered beneath the perfume and wine.

Nyla kept her movements measured. Performers were meant to move gracefully, not look like they were mapping escape routes.

Marisol had done her part—faking the invitation, rerouting her ID through the performers' registry. Tavi was somewhere in the rafters, probably chewing on her nails and whispering obscenities into her comm. They'd come here to stop Ardelia's broadcast. To find the signal core and cut it before she could use the Prime Note to enslave every living frequency on earth.

But as Nyla stepped onto the stage, she realized how far they were from subtlety.

The centerpiece of the gala wasn't the guests, or even the music. It was the tower of glass that rose from the center of the floor like a monument. Inside, suspended in a field of pulsing light, were the Prime conduits—the same resonance cylinders she'd seen in the vault. Only now they were awake, vibrating with energy that made her teeth ache.

Ardelia stood before them.

She wore white, the kind of white that made her seem untouchable. Her hair gleamed silver under the stage lights. Every step she took radiated command. The crowd parted instinctively, a living tide yielding to its gravity.

Nyla stayed in the wings, eyes fixed on her. Beside Ardelia, two enforcers guided a figure toward the stage. Nyla's heart stuttered when she saw Kian.

He was bound from throat to ankle with glimmerwire, thicker than before, glowing with interference fields that shifted in color. A sonic dampener circled his neck, pulsing every few seconds with sharp bursts of null frequency. He moved like he'd been hollowed out, every step deliberate, precise, restrained.

The audience whispered, a thousand frequencies overlapping in intrigue. They didn't recognize him for what he was. Not yet.

Ardelia raised her hand, and the sound in the room flattened to silence. The quartet stopped mid-bow, the chatter cut off mid-syllable. It wasn't command. It was control.

"My family," she began, her voice carrying effortlessly, rich and warm. "Tonight we stand at the threshold of something long promised and long feared. The dawn of unity."

Nyla felt the words crawl under her skin.

"For centuries, we have lived divided," Ardelia continued. "Sound and Silence. Flesh and void. Creation and restraint. We called it balance. But balance is weakness disguised as peace."

The audience murmured. A few Resonants shifted uncomfortably. Others nodded, eager.

Ardelia's gaze swept the crowd, her smile sharp. "The Houses were never meant to exist apart. We are one frequency fractured into four. Tonight, that fracture ends. Tonight, we merge."

The lights dimmed. The glass tower behind her pulsed brighter, the conduits flaring one by one. The low hum Nyla had carried in her blood since the vault grew louder, vibrating in sympathy.

Ardelia gestured toward Kian. "The House of Silence sought to contain us. To neutralize what they feared. But we have learned their secret."

The enforcers shoved Kian to his knees.

"Silence is not death," Ardelia said, stepping closer to him. "It is potential. It is the pause before the song."

She placed her hand over his throat. The air rippled. The dampener at his neck responded, sparking with interference, and he flinched but didn't look away.

"With his resonance and ours combined," she said, "we will summon the Prime Note not as weapon, but as will. No more hunger. No more secrecy. No more difference between Resonant and Damper. One harmony. One law."

Her hand tightened on his throat. "Mine."

The crowd erupted in applause.

Nyla's nails dug into her palms. She wanted to scream. Instead, she adjusted the comm in her ear. "Marisol," she whispered. "Tell me you're in position."

Marisol's voice came back low and strained. "I'm trying, but the security field's locked tighter than I thought. The Note's energy is feeding the grid."

"Tavi?"

"Don't ask me questions right now," Tavi hissed. "I'm climbing, and my legs are doing that shake thing they do before I make bad decisions."

Nyla's attention snapped back to the stage. Ardelia moved toward the console at the center of the platform. Her fingers danced over the controls, and a holographic interface bloomed in the air. The waveform from the vault unfolded above them, golden and terrible.

She looked divine standing there, her face illuminated by power, her eyes reflecting the pattern like molten glass.

"Tonight," Ardelia said, "the Houses return to their source. The sound that began us will bind us. The Prime Note will rewrite what we are. No more blood. No more shadows. Only resonance."

The crowd rose to its feet, the collective hum swelling as their frequencies synced to her rhythm. Nyla could feel it through the floor, through her skin. Ardelia was using them as amplifiers.

Kian met Nyla's eyes across the hall. The restraint at his neck flickered, blue light sputtering. For a second, his silence pulsed against hers—familiar, steady, deliberate. She felt him, faint but certain.

He was still fighting.

Ardelia turned to her audience, arms raised. "Witness the future."

The Prime conduits flared again, each one aligning to a new key. The sound that followed wasn't sound at all—

it was the memory of creation, a vibration that bypassed the ear and lived straight in the blood.

Every vampire in the room stiffened. The Resonants gasped as their pulses synced to the Note, pupils dilating. The air thickened with pressure. Nyla could barely breathe.

The Note was rewriting them.

She gripped the edge of the lighting rig, holding herself upright. Across the hall, Kian strained against his restraints, muscles shaking, the glimmerwire burning against his skin.

Ardelia's voice merged with the music. "Sound is power. Silence is control. Together, they are obedience."

Nyla's pulse thundered. The lights blurred. The pendant at her throat burned like fire. She could feel the Prime Note pulling at her resonance, trying to swallow it, to make her part of the choir.

She refused.

Her own hum rose unbidden, low at first, then higher, clashing with the Prime Note's perfect symmetry. The vibration sparked through the metal railing, across the lights, into the walls.

Marisol's voice crackled in her ear. "Whatever you're doing, keep doing it. The system's destabilizing. If I can overload the amplifier network, we can—"

Her voice vanished in static.

Nyla's vision dimmed. The stage lights pulsed brighter, reflecting in Ardelia's eyes.

The Maestra smiled. She had known Nyla would come, and she had planned for it.

The crowd's hum rose, shifting from awe to frenzy. The Prime Note filled the space like a tide, swallowing everything that wasn't submission.

Nyla pressed a hand to her chest, gasping, her heart beating too fast to keep up. She could feel her blood singing in two pitches struggling to decide which one it belonged to.

Above her, lightning flashed through the glass ceiling, painting the city white. The gala was no longer a performance. It was a ritual.

# XV

The lights dimmed to a twilight hue. A ripple moved through the crowd — the hush before revelation. Above the stage, holographic waveforms spun like halos, refracting light in a thousand directions. Cameras from every House channel floated through the air, recording history in real time.

Ardelia stood at the center of it all, her arms outstretched like a conductor invoking creation itself. The Prime Note shimmered above her, a perfect golden thread stretched across the room.

Nyla, hidden in the wings, could feel it crawling beneath her skin — that terrible vibration, familiar and wrong. It reminded her of the vault, of those humming cylinders, of her own blood shaking in time with something older than memory.

She had minutes. Maybe seconds.

Tavi's whisper crackled through her comm, faint and terrified. "Stage vents are open. I've got access to the soundboard feed. You sure about this, boss?"

"No," Nyla breathed. "Do it anyway."

Marisol's voice followed, steady but strained. "The Prime network's tied directly into her frequency core. Once you touch that signal, you'll be feeding it through yourself."

"I know."

"Then you'll have to survive it long enough to stop her."

Nyla stepped out of the shadows, each footfall swallowed by the swelling sound. The audience barely noticed her. They were already swaying — eyes unfocused, pulses syncing with Ardelia's rhythm.

The Maestra saw her. A faint smile curved her lips. "Ah," she said into the mic, her voice resonating through the walls, "the missing note arrives."

Every head turned.

Nyla took the stage slowly, the pendant at her throat flickering with pale light. "You're playing the wrong song," she said.

Ardelia tilted her head. "And yet you came to hear it."

Her fingers brushed the console. The sound deepened, spreading like honey through the air. The crowd trembled.

Nyla's blood thrummed in answer. The Prime Note wanted her. It reached through every body in the hall to get to her. She let it pull her closer. Then she reached for the spare mic stand and pressed her palm to the base, letting her own frequency slide into the current.

The system recognized her immediately. The waveform above the stage flared red.

Gasps rippled through the crowd.

"What are you doing?" Ardelia's voice cut through the resonance, sharp and commanding.

"Finishing the set," Nyla said.

The sound changed. Her modified frequency slipped into the mix. The perfect symmetry fractured, branching into something wild, unpredictable.

Where Ardelia's music had been divine order, Nyla's was rebellion.

It started soft—a tremor under the bass. A heartbeat layered with human imperfection.

Then it grew.

The Prime Note faltered.

The crowd's sway shifted from reverence to rapture. Laughter, gasps, cries — emotion exploding like sparks. Some collapsed into ecstasy, others screamed. The air became thick with heat, the scent of sweat and iron rising like incense.

Nyla's voice cut through it all. She wasn't speaking words anymore. She was channeling raw resonance, sound turned to touch. The walls pulsed. The lights bent.

Ardelia's calm cracked. "You're destabilizing them," she hissed, turning dials, her hands moving fast. "You think you can outsing God?"

"I'm not outsinging you," Nyla said, eyes blazing. "I'm reminding them what freedom sounds like."

The music became war.

Ardelia's hands slammed the console, and the Prime Note surged back, drowning out everything else. A wall of pure sound hit Nyla like a shockwave, throwing her against the rigging. The crowd screamed as the resonance deepened into agony.

Nyla rose. Blood streaked her lip. She met Ardelia's gaze through the haze of vibrating light.

Then the Maestra raised her hand.

Silence.

Every sound collapsed at once. The room imploded into a vacuum of nothing. Breath stopped. Heartbeats faltered. The audience froze mid-motion, expressions locked between awe and terror.

The quiet hurt more than any scream.

Nyla staggered, clutching her chest. Her resonance tried to escape, but the silence swallowed it whole. It was Ardelia's true weapon — the void she'd stolen from the House of Silence and turned into art.

"You wanted to be the voice of change," Ardelia said, her tone calm, merciless. "Now listen to what you've done."

Nyla's body trembled. Her pulse slowed. The silence pressed down harder, crushing her lungs. She could feel it trying to erase her—to still the vibration in her blood.

But beneath the suffocation, something inside her refused to die.

The Prime Note still lived in her veins, bound to her resonance. She let her body go slack, surrendering for just a heartbeat. Then she focused — drawing the hum inward instead of out. Feeding it through her core, amplifying it, shaping it.

Ardelia took a step forward, hand outstretched. "Kneel."

Nyla smiled faintly. "No."

She released it.

The sound burst from her chest like lightning. It wasn't melody—it was fury.

The silence shattered.

Ardelia's head snapped back as the blast hit. The crowd convulsed. Every pane of glass in the hall fractured into powder. Lights swung wildly, spraying sparks. The floor rippled like water as frequencies collided — resonance against void.

The storm became physical.

Nyla's hum met Ardelia's silence in a clash that ripped through the structure, bending metal beams and warping concrete. The chandeliers exploded. Shockwaves tore through the audience. Resonants dropped to their knees, their bodies vibrating too fast to hold shape.

Marisol's voice screamed through the comm, then cut off.

Tavi's laughter crackled faintly before static devoured it.

Nyla kept singing. She couldn't stop. The music poured out of her like blood, raw and endless. She felt everything — the crowd's pain, their euphoria, their terror. The Prime Note wasn't controlling them anymore. It was *consuming* them.

Ardelia roared, countering with another surge of silence so dense it crushed the air from the room.

The collision was cataclysmic.

Sound became weapon. Silence became blade. The two forces met at the center of the hall, spiraling into a cyclone of light and shadow. The walls cracked. The glass dome above them split open, letting in the storm outside. Rain fell sideways into the chaos, hissing as it struck the charged air.

Kian's restraints snapped. He crawled toward the stage through the debris, fighting to reach her. "Nyla!"

She turned her head just as the final wave hit.

The resonance burst outward, expanding like a detonation. For a single, blinding instant, the world became all color and pressure — music and stillness fused into one impossible moment.

Then everything went white.

When the light faded, the gala was gone.

Half the hall lay in ruin. Glass, bodies, and instruments all scattered in silence. The air still trembled with the aftermath.

Nyla lay amid the wreckage, smoke curling from her fingertips, her eyes reflecting the broken lights.

Ardelia was nowhere to be seen.

The silence that followed was wrong. Not peaceful, not stunned—predatory.

Kian pushed himself upright, glass splintering beneath his palms. His throat burned where the dampener had been, skin raw, the faint taste of copper coating his tongue. The air around him still shimmered with residual charge. Every breath came with the faintest echo, like the sound had forgotten how to die.

He blinked through the haze. The grand hall of Arista was unrecognizable — chandeliers collapsed like melted bones, marble cracked, walls buckled. The storm outside had slipped through the broken dome, rain hissing as it struck live wires and blood.

Tavi was the first to move. She crawled out from beneath a shattered lighting rig, glitter streaked with soot, her eyes glassy but alert. "Still breathing," she croaked. "Didn't see that on tonight's setlist."

Marisol staggered into view next, clutching her shoulder where a shard of glass had punched through. The wound was already knitting itself closed, the skin glowing faintly. She looked around, her expression tight. "Is she alive?"

Kian turned toward the center of the room.

Nyla stood amidst the wreckage like the eye of the storm. Her dress was torn, soaked in crimson and rain, the pendant at her throat flickering like a dying star. The air around her pulsed — visible waves rippling outward, distorting the space they passed through.

She wasn't humming, but the room still vibrated with her.

"Nyla." Kian's voice cracked.

She turned slowly. Her eyes gleamed faint gold, the color of the Prime Note itself. Her hair clung to her face, her expression unreadable.

He stepped closer. "It's over."

"No," she said softly, tilting her head as if listening to something distant. "It's still playing."

Tavi wiped her forehead, smearing blood and glitter. "Yeah, that's great, babe, but could you maybe turn the apocalypse volume down? My ears are doing the drum solo from hell."

Marisol limped forward, eyes scanning the fractured stage. "She's right. The frequency's still active. It's faint, but it's everywhere — in the walls, the wiring, the water. It's like the city's humming along with it."

Nyla smiled faintly. "Can you feel it?"

Kian hesitated. "What did you do?"

"I didn't stop it," she said. "I changed it."

The wind surged through the broken dome, carrying her hair back. She looked alive in a way that frightened him. Her skin glowed with faint light, the kind that pulsed in rhythm with her heartbeat.

She stepped forward, bare feet cutting on the glass. The wounds closed before she took the next step. The hum around her grew stronger, alive and electric, making the air shimmer.

Marisol stared. "Your resonance—it's evolved."

Nyla laughed, the sound soft but heavy with charge. "No. It's free."

Kian reached her. "You can't hold that kind of power. It'll burn you from the inside."

She looked at him, eyes still glowing. "Then let it."

Lightning cracked through the open roof, the thunder following a beat too late. The entire room trembled in response, as if the storm itself had answered her.

Tavi whistled low. "Okay, so we're just not pretending to be mortal anymore? Good to know."

Nyla turned in a slow circle, scanning the wreckage. "Where is she?"

Ardelia's absence was a hole in the air. The woman who had commanded a House, who had orchestrated a symphony of control, was gone. Not a sound, not a shadow, not a trace. Only the faintest imprint of her resonance remained — a whisper buried beneath Nyla's own.

"She couldn't have survived that," Marisol said.

Kian's expression stayed flat. "She's not the kind to die quietly."

Nyla crouched, running her fingers across the ruined stage. The floor still vibrated faintly — Ardelia's signature, muted and fading, but not gone. It threaded through the marble like a vein. She closed her eyes, tracing the pulse through the cracks.

"She went below."

Marisol frowned. "There's nothing below the main hall but the control levels."

"No," Nyla murmured. "There's always something below."

She stood again, her movements fluid, graceful in a way that made even the air hesitate. Her voice carried the weight of two worlds. "She built this place on the bones of the first resonance chamber. The original foundation. That's where she'd go — where the Note began."

Tavi kicked a broken microphone across the floor. "Fantastic. Basement showdown with the vampire version of Beethoven. Love it."

Nyla didn't smile. Her gaze drifted toward the stairwell at the far end of the ruined hall, where the shadows seemed too still.

Kian reached for her arm, but the moment he touched her, static leapt between them. He hissed, pulling back.

She glanced at him, guilt flickering across her face for just a heartbeat. "I can't control it yet."

"That's exactly why you shouldn't chase her."

She met his eyes. "And if I don't?"

Kian didn't answer. He didn't have to. The air still tasted of ash and lightning, of something unfinished.

Marisol retrieved her scanner from a fallen beam, shaking dust off it. The display flickered but stabilized. "The energy signatures are spiking again. Whatever she left down there, it's active. We don't have long before the Council picks up the signal."

Tavi stretched, wincing as her shoulder cracked. "You know what I'm hearing? Road trip. Underground edition."

Kian rubbed the back of his neck, still staring at Nyla. "You'll burn yourself out."

"Then I'll burn her first."

The words came quiet, but they were final.

Rain dripped from the broken ceiling, pooling around their feet. The reflections shimmered with faint gold, like the Prime Note still lingered in the puddles.

Nyla stared into it, mesmerized by the ripples. The power coursing through her veins pulsed brighter, its rhythm syncing with the storm. She felt it in every nerve, a living symphony. It hurt, but it felt holy.

She loved it.

And part of her loved that she loved it.

Marisol pressed a hand to her chest. "Your resonance is bleeding into the environment. You need to ground yourself before you overload."

Nyla exhaled, eyes half-lidded. "I am grounded."

The lights flickered above them, answering her heartbeat.

Kian stepped closer again, voice low. "You don't have to become her to stop her."

Nyla smiled, small and unsteady. "Maybe that's the only way."

A gust of wind tore through the broken roof, scattering dust and debris like ash. The hall seemed to hum with anticipation, as though the House itself was listening.

Marisol pocketed her scanner, grim. "Then we'd better find her before the rest of the Houses do."

Nyla nodded once, turning toward the stairwell. The stormlight caught her eyes, gold burning through the dark.

Behind her, the others followed—limping, bleeding, alive.

The House of Sound, once a temple, now felt like a tomb. Its walls still trembled faintly, carrying the echo of what had been born here tonight.

# XVI

The air changed first. That subtle shift before the storm when the pressure drops and every nerve in your body goes still, waiting.

Marisol stopped mid-scan. "Do you feel that?"

Kian tensed, eyes narrowing. "It's not the Note."

Nyla turned toward the stairwell. The shadows at the base of the broken hall seemed to ripple, the darkness deepening until it swallowed the light around it.

Something moved within it. Slow. Purposeful.

When the first vibration hit, it wasn't sound. It was weight—a force pressing down through the air like the entire House had taken a breath and refused to exhale.

Tavi's voice cracked. "Oh no. No, no, no."

Ardelia stepped into view.

Her white gown was torn, streaked with soot and blood, but she walked like nothing had touched her. Her skin glowed faintly beneath the grime, veins threaded with light, her eyes twin fractures of silver. Her voice, when it came, wasn't amplified — it simply filled the space.

"You should have stayed beneath me, child."

Before Nyla could answer, the Maestra raised her hand. The air folded inward.

The blast of force hit Nyla square in the chest. She flew backward into a collapsed column, the impact cracking stone. The sound was deafening.

Marisol dove behind the remains of a speaker tower. Tavi cursed, scrambling for cover.

Kian was already moving, but Ardelia flicked two fingers and the floor itself rippled, knocking him off balance.

"You were meant to inherit the world I built," Ardelia said, stepping through the ruin. "Not destroy it."

Nyla coughed, pushing herself up, blood running down her chin. "You built a cage."

"I built order."

"You built silence."

Ardelia smiled, and the world seemed to dim in deference. "Then let me teach you how to live in it."

She struck again, a surge of resonance so concentrated it warped the air into ribbons of heat. Nyla countered instinctively, her frequency flaring, gold light exploding from her hands. The collision bent the space between them, a visible distortion, wind whipping outward in waves.

The two forces clashed—gold against silver, resonance against void—throwing sparks that clung to the air like fireflies before bursting into miniature thunderclaps.

Ardelia moved like a dancer. Every gesture controlled. Every sound she summoned shaped into a weapon. A note sliced past Nyla's shoulder, sharp as a blade, carving a line through the wall behind her.

Nyla ducked, rolling across the fractured floor. The hum in her blood screamed for release. She planted one hand on the ground and released a pulse of energy. The floor split, light spilling through the cracks like molten glass.

Ardelia laughed. "Beautiful. But you still don't understand what you're wielding."

"I don't need to understand it," Nyla said, teeth bared. "I *am* it."

She struck again.

The sound ripped through the air, a single sustained note that resonated through every shard of glass left in the room. The fragments rose around them, suspended midair, each one humming in harmony with her voice.

Ardelia didn't flinch. She lifted her arm, palm out, and everything stilled. The floating shards dropped as gravity reasserted itself. The silence that followed was suffocating.

"You think music is freedom," Ardelia said. "But it's obedience. Every note obeys the laws of harmony. Even chaos needs a key."

She lunged forward, closing the distance between them. The impact was brutal—two frequencies colliding, the world twisting around them as energy bled into the walls.

Nyla hit the ground hard, her vision flashing white. The hum in her veins faltered, splintered, screamed.

Ardelia stood over her, voice soft, almost mournful. "I made you to be more than hunger."

Nyla spat blood, her voice shaking but defiant. "You didn't make me."

Ardelia lifted her hand for the final strike — the one that would shatter her resonance completely.

That's when Kian moved.

He slammed into Ardelia from the side, shoulder first, the impact throwing her off balance for a fraction of a second. Enough.

Ardelia snarled, her resonance flaring bright, forcing him back. "You again."

He planted his feet, wiped blood from his mouth. "Miss me?"

"You can't kill what you were designed to serve," she said.

"Then maybe I'll rewrite the design."

He reached for Nyla, pressing his hand against her chest. The contact burned — her resonance was unstable, wild — but he didn't let go.

"Nyla," he said, voice steady despite the chaos. "Listen to me."

She gasped, trembling. "I can't—"

"Yes, you can. You're not fighting her. You're fighting *the Note.* Let me in."

She met his gaze, eyes wild, and nodded once.

Their frequencies collided — her golden resonance against his cold, steady counterfrequency — and for a heartbeat, it was agony. Then it balanced.

The storm around them slowed, the debris hanging midair. Ardelia froze mid-step, her expression faltering for the first time.

"What are you doing?" she hissed.

"Conducting," Kian said.

The Note inside Nyla shifted, no longer a weapon straining to explode but a current flowing outward. The energy that had threatened to consume her began to realign, shaped by Kian's counterfrequency.

Her breath steadied. The golden light around her deepened, layered with streaks of blue — his color. The two resonances intertwined, singing in harmony.

The Prime Note itself began to change.

It was no longer a single, devastating pitch. It became many — overlapping tones, imperfect but alive. The vibration filled the ruined hall, shaking dust from the rafters, echoing through the cracked stone like the pulse of something reborn.

Ardelia screamed.

"No! You'll undo everything!"

She threw another wave of force, but it broke against the harmony surrounding them. The bridge they'd created absorbed it, redirecting the energy upward through the fractured dome.

The sound reached the storm above, and the sky answered. Lightning struck the dome's edge, spiderwebbing through the shattered glass. Rain poured in sheets, drenching the ruins.

Nyla's voice rose higher, the power coursing through her like electricity. It hurt — gods, it *hurt* — but it was beautiful. She felt everything: the pulse of every Resonant still breathing in the city, the cry of the bay, the hum of the air itself.

And beneath it all, the fragile thread of her own immortality unraveling.

Her resonance flared too bright. She could feel it burning her from the inside, stripping her apart note by note. But she didn't stop.

Kian gripped her hand tighter. His frequency steadied hers, holding the bridge open. "Nyla, it's working."

"I can't hold it much longer," she gasped.

"You don't have to."

He stepped in front of her, shielding her from the next burst of Ardelia's fury. The Maestra's power slammed into him like a hammer, but the counterfrequency held. His body shook under the strain, veins glowing faint blue.

Ardelia's face twisted, rage and despair breaking through her composure. "You can't erase me."

Nyla rose behind him, light bleeding from her eyes, her voice barely more than a whisper. "I don't have to."

The bridge flared, pure sound and silence braided into one perfect moment. The energy expanded outward, washing over everything — dissolving the residual Note, cleansing the static.

Ardelia's scream cut off mid-breath.

When the light faded, she was gone.

The hall fell still again, the storm outside slowing to a drizzle.

Kian dropped to his knees, the glow fading from his skin. Nyla collapsed beside him, her breath shallow, her pulse a faint vibration.

He caught her before she hit the ground. Her eyes flickered open, the gold dimming to gray.

"Did we—" she started, voice hoarse.

He nodded. "You turned it into something else."

She smiled weakly. "A bridge."

Then her head fell against his shoulder, her resonance fading into silence.

The rain kept falling, steady and soft, carrying the echo of what they had created. As Kian held her, the world hummed again, gentle this time. Not in obedience, but in awe.

Kian held her closer. The heat radiating from her skin was fading, her glow dimming with every breath. The rain poured through the shattered dome, soaking them both, streaking the marble in gray and silver.

She wasn't moving.

"Nyla." His voice broke on her name. "Hey. Come on."

Her eyes fluttered halfway open, unfocused. A faint hum escaped her lips—barely there, a dying chord. The bridge she'd built still shimmered faintly above them, threads of light rippling through the air like the afterglow of something holy.

It was unraveling.

The gold tones dissolved into blue, then white, then nothing. The air fell still. The rain quieted. For the first time since the Note had awakened, the world was quiet—real quiet, not the void Ardelia commanded, but peace.

Marisol limped closer, eyes wide, soaked to the bone. Her scanner flickered, its display filled with unreadable static. "Her frequency's collapsing," she whispered. "It's burning out."

Tavi stumbled forward, glass crunching beneath her boots. "No, no, she just needs to rest. Right? People pass out after apocalypses all the time."

Kian didn't look up. His thumb brushed across Nyla's cheek. Her skin was too cool. "She's not people."

"Then fix her," Tavi snapped. Her voice cracked, high and raw. "You always fix things. So fix her!"

He shook his head slowly. "I can't."

Nyla stirred, her voice so faint it was barely a vibration. "You can," she murmured.

Kian's breath hitched. "You shouldn't be talking."

She smiled weakly. "You shouldn't be worrying."

The sound of her voice vibrated through his chest. It wasn't music—it was memory, resonance reduced to human fragility. Her immortality was fading, her connection to the Prime Note untethered. And yet she looked lighter than she ever had.

"Do you feel it?" she whispered.

He blinked away rain and tears alike. "Feel what?"

"The quiet," she said. "It's... beautiful."

Kian swallowed hard, shaking his head. "No. You don't get to love this. Not now."

Her laugh was soft, barely audible. "Always the serious one."

Marisol crouched beside them, her voice trembling. "Her pulse is slowing, but it's still there. The resonance isn't gone, it's just—"

"Changing," Nyla finished for her, her tone threaded with awe. "I can feel it. The bridge... it's holding."

Kian glanced around. The air shimmered faintly, as if her final act hadn't vanished at all but spread invisibly through the city. Somewhere out there, he could *feel* it too—the pulse of life returning to the Houses, the silence lifting, resonance redistributing.

Nyla's eyes found his again. "If this works... they'll all hear it. Not as control. As choice."

His throat tightened. "You sound like her."

Her lips curved faintly. "Then maybe she wasn't all wrong."

Lightning flashed again, painting the hall in pale light. Kian could see it then—her skin fracturing with faint luminescent lines, veins glowing briefly before fading away. Every piece of her was dissolving into vibration.

"No." He tightened his grip, desperate. "You're not going anywhere."

"I think I already am."

Tavi wiped her face with the back of her hand, tears streaking through grime. "Don't you dare pull a tragic hero thing right now. I will bring you back and make you listen to my mixtape for eternity."

Nyla's faint laugh sounded like the ghost of a melody. "That's crueler than death."

Marisol stood, backing up as her scanner stabilized for the first time since the explosion. "Oh my god..."

"What?" Kian demanded.

"The bridge isn't gone," she said, eyes wide. "It's *her*. She's phasing into it."

The floor began to vibrate again—softly, like the heartbeat of something massive beneath them. Threads of gold light rose from Nyla's body, curling upward, diffusing into the air. Her resonance wasn't dying. It was ascending.

Kian held her tighter, trying to keep her anchored. "Nyla, don't."

She reached up, her palm against his cheek. "You helped me turn it into something better. Let it be."

"I can't lose you."

"You never will." Her voice thinned into a whisper. "I'm part of everything now."

He shook his head violently. "That's not enough."

Her smile was sad and tender all at once. "It's everything."

Light enveloped her. It wasn't harsh or blinding—just warmth, deep and golden, spilling across the ruined hall. Kian felt it hum against his skin, soft at first, then pulsing, wrapping around his heartbeat. For a moment, he could swear he heard her laugh inside the sound.

Then she was gone.

The light faded slowly, leaving only the rain, the broken hall, and three survivors standing in the echo of a miracle.

Tavi covered her mouth, silent tears cutting through the dirt on her face. Marisol wiped her eyes and whispered, "She did it."

Kian didn't move. His hand was still outstretched where she'd been, the air vibrating faintly against his fingertips.

Somewhere far above, the clouds began to break, streaks of dawn filtering through. The storm had finally exhausted itself.

In the distance, faint and almost human, a new sound rose—a hum, soft and clear, threading through the city like a heartbeat shared by everyone who could still feel it.

# XVII

The wave began as a shimmer. A faint, invisible ripple that drifted from the ruins of Arista House and rolled through Miami like a tide no one could see coming. It threaded through the streets, into the high-rises and basements, through the sea walls and storm drains. Every signal, every broadcast, every heartbeat—alive or undead—vibrated to its pulse.

Traffic lights flickered. Radios hissed. Every speaker in every club cut out, then hummed softly with a tone that wasn't quite sound, wasn't quite silence. It was both.

Then came the shift.

The vampires felt it first. The Resonants froze mid-breath, eyes wide as the old, flat hum in their blood broke apart and reassembled. It didn't hurt. Not like feeding or starving. It was… *awakening.*

A thousand frequencies corrected themselves at once. The old static that had insulated their minds dissolved, and for the first time in centuries, they felt *everything.*

Joy. Hunger. Sorrow. Regret.

Some laughed. Others wept. One collapsed in the street, clutching his chest because the sound of his own heartbeat was too beautiful to bear.

In the waterfront district, an entire club went still mid-beat, dancers and DJs and drinkers frozen as the wave rolled through. A moment later, the air was alive with applause, laughter, and sobs—raw and human and divine all at once.

On rooftops, Resonants looked up toward the broken sky and swore they could hear her singing still.

The sound lingered in the air like the last breath of a storm—thin, high, and radiant. It wound through the wrecked skyline, slipping between towers and radio masts, echoing in the steel and glass. Every surface vibrated faintly, humming with what felt like memory.

Across the city, vampires stood motionless in the rain. Some tilted their heads, eyes closed, as if listening for something half-forgotten. Others fell to their knees, overcome not by pain but by a sensation they hadn't known in decades: warmth.

For the first time since the founding of the Houses, there was no single hum uniting them. Each pulse was unique. Each resonance carried its own rhythm. It should have been chaos. It should have torn them apart.

Instead, it harmonized.

Every windowpane and puddle reflected a thousand flickering lights. The streets glowed faintly gold where the sound wave had passed, and the air felt heavier—not with fear, but with possibility.

A young Resonant woman on the causeway laughed suddenly, startling the humans near her. The sound wasn't controlled or deliberate. It was just laughter—messy, alive, and echoing off the concrete. Others joined her, a ripple of disbelief giving way to joy.

In Little Havana, an old vampire who'd lived too long in silence sat beside a mural and wept, clutching the faded photograph of a daughter he could finally remember. On Ocean Drive, two fledglings who'd once fed together out of instinct now held each other, trembling, because the blood no longer dulled what they felt—it amplified it.

The storm broke over the bay, scattering light across the waves. The reflection shimmered gold, then blue, then gold again, as if the water itself was trying to hum along.

And through it all, faint and unending, that song persisted—Nyla's resonance woven into the pulse of the city, her final note rippling outward until even the wind seemed to keep her tempo.

Somewhere high above, lightning forked one last time and vanished into clear sky. The night surrendered to morning.

Below, in the remnants of Arista's great hall, Kian stood among the ruins. The storm had broken completely now, the clouds torn apart by dawn.

The Prime Note had faded from the air, replaced by something quieter, something alive. The world didn't hum with control anymore—it breathed.

Marisol sat on the edge of the shattered stage, staring out at the skyline where the sunrise cut through the mist. "They're... changing," she said softly. "All of them. It's like a reset. Their resonance has been rewritten."

Tavi crouched beside a puddle, her reflection rippling. "I just saw a guy on the street smile at the sun. A vampire smiling at the *sun,* Marisol. I thought I was hallucinating."

Kian didn't speak. He could still feel her. Not in the air this time, but inside his own chest—an echo, steady as a second pulse. The bridge hadn't vanished. It was humming quietly through him.

He looked up at the sky, where light filtered down like strands of gold silk, and whispered, "Where are you?"

The question dissolved into the wind, but something in the air seemed to answer. Not a voice. Not even a sound. Just a pulse — faint, steady, deliberate — brushing the edges of his awareness like fingertips tracing skin.

The dawn spilled through the broken dome in ribbons, each one catching the drifting dust and fractured glass until it looked like the air itself was breathing. Kian tilted his head, closing his eyes, listening the way only a Damper could — not for what was loud, but for what refused to die.

There it was again.

A hum. Subtle. Off-key, but alive.

He could feel it threading through the ruins, coiling around the shattered beams, the fallen instruments, the soaked marble floor where she'd stood. It wasn't the Prime Note—that perfect, crushing sound that had consumed everything. This was smaller, flawed, human. It was *her*.

Kian stepped forward, the water lapping around his boots. Each ripple carried a faint vibration that crawled up through the soles of his feet and into his chest. His pulse answered it instinctively, syncing with the rhythm like a duet across the void.

Marisol and Tavi had gone quiet behind him, sensing it too. Neither spoke. The air was too fragile for words.

Kian sank to his knees where the stage used to be. The marble beneath his hands was warm, faintly thrumming, as if the building itself remembered her touch. He closed his eyes and let the sound envelop him—low, steady, filled with impossible clarity.

He remembered the way she'd stood there moments before the end, the way the light had caught her eyes, the way her voice had turned war into art. He remembered her laugh – defiant, reckless, alive – when she'd realized what the Note could become. And now, even in absence, he could feel the echo of that moment hanging in the air.

"You're not gone," he whispered.

A gust of wind swept through the broken roof, scattering rain across his face. It tasted faintly metallic, and when he exhaled, the droplets around him rippled outward, tiny circles of gold light chasing one another across the puddles.

He reached out, his palm hovering above the water. It quivered beneath him, reacting to something unseen.

The hum rose in pitch, surrounding him completely. The air vibrated until it became light, and the light folded inward until it became silence again.

For a heartbeat, he thought he saw her — not standing, not spectral, just movement in the gold, a curve of light shaped like her smile.

Then the warmth faded, leaving only the rain and his reflection.

Kian lowered his head, his voice barely audible. "Come back."

The hum pulsed one final time, soft and deliberate, like a promise.

And somewhere beyond sound, beyond the city, beyond the waking world—

Nyla opened her eyes to light.

It wasn't sunlight. It wasn't warmth, or even brightness as she had known it. It was vibration made visible, the entire world composed of sound that shimmered, fluid and alive. Each breath she took became a ripple through the landscape. Each thought cast its own reflection.

She stood—or maybe she floated—in a field of endless resonance. The horizon moved like the surface of water, its color shifting with every pulse of her heart.

For a moment, there was nothing but silence. The kind that came after the song, not before it.

Then a voice. Soft, layered, familiar.

"You always had a gift for ruining perfect symmetry."

Nyla turned. Ardelia stood behind her, radiant and calm, her form outlined in silver threads of vibration. She looked different—older and younger all at once, as if time had finally let go of her.

"You're not real," Nyla said quietly.

"I'm not alive," Ardelia corrected. "There's a difference."

Nyla's pulse quickened. "What is this place?"

Ardelia's eyes moved across the glowing horizon. "It's what remains when resonance burns too bright. The space between frequency and form. You reached for the bridge, and it answered."

"I died?"

"Not quite."

Nyla looked down. Her body shimmered faintly, more energy than flesh. Each movement left a trail of light that took a moment too long to fade.

Ardelia stepped closer, her expression unreadable. "You remade the Note. You didn't destroy it—you *rewrote* it. The bridge you built connects every living frequency now. Vampires, humans, silents, sound—all of them. But bridges require anchors."

Nyla frowned. "Anchors?"

"Someone has to hold the resonance steady," Ardelia said. "Keep the frequencies from collapsing again. That's what the Prime Note was meant to be—a conductor of equilibrium. It needs a guardian."

Nyla's chest tightened. "And that's me."

"You were chosen the moment you touched it."

Nyla turned her face toward the horizon, the endless hum vibrating through her bones. "And if I stay here?"

"Then the balance remains intact," Ardelia said. "The bridge stays strong. The world keeps singing."

"And if I go back?"

Ardelia smiled faintly. "Then the bridge falters. The world learns dissonance again. But it won't collapse. Not entirely. You'll keep your power—but you'll carry its echo. The bridge will live *through* you, not beyond you. Every heartbeat will cost you a little more of the equilibrium you gave them."

Nyla's throat ached. "So either I stay and keep the world in harmony forever… or I go back and live, knowing I'll always be half of something unfinished."

Ardelia nodded. "Every song ends, Nyla. But the beauty is in the ending."

Silence stretched between them, warm and infinite.

For a long moment, Nyla listened—to the pulse of the bridge, to the resonance of millions of lives now waking to a world that finally *felt.* The sound was chaotic, uneven, imperfect.

It was alive.

She smiled. "Then I think it's time the world learned to sing for itself."

Ardelia's eyes softened. "You always did prefer the noise."

Light rose around Nyla's feet, spiraling upward, tugging gently. The vibration increased, deepening into a tone that felt like both farewell and promise.

She looked once more at Ardelia. "Will I see you again?"

Ardelia's smile was quiet and eternal. "Every time someone listens."

The light consumed her. The world folded back into itself, one shimmering chord collapsing into silence.

For an instant, there was nothing but the endless vibration of being. No pain, no sound, no body. The bridge she had created expanded outward, connecting everything. She could feel it stretching across the city, across every beating heart and trembling frequency.

Every vampire who had ever silenced their hunger.

Every human who had ever felt the echo of something more.

Every note that had ever been played and forgotten.

They were all inside her, their frequencies harmonizing into something greater. She wasn't dissolving—she was *everywhere.*

The light was warm, alive, infinite. It wasn't blindness. It was understanding.

She drifted through it, weightless, her thoughts stretched into chords. The rain over Miami became percussion. The thunder rolled in bass tones beneath it. Every laugh, every sob, every heartbeat in the city added a new texture to the music.

It was all so clear. Every soul a frequency. Every frequency a life. And yet, even in that perfect resonance, she felt the tether. A single, quiet counterpoint running through the storm of sound. Familiar, grounding, steady.

Kian's presence glowed like blue heat against the gold of her own frequency, a melody that refused to fade. Through the bridge she could *feel* him—the steadiness of his heartbeat, the tremor in his breath, the ache that threaded every time he said her name.

It called to her.

She drifted toward it, through the veil of light and vibration, through the thousands of sounds still echoing her name. Her form began to take shape again, threads of resonance condensing into warmth, into breath, into body.

The bridge resisted, not cruelly, but protectively. It pulsed around her, whispering in its own strange way: *Stay.*

She hesitated.

Beyond the light, she could sense peace — the true kind, vast and endless, where nothing hurt and everything was music. But within it, she could feel distance growing, the gap between her and the world she'd saved widening.

She heard Kian's voice through the static, soft and fractured.

*Nyla... please...*

Her decision was immediate. She reached for the sound.

The bridge shook as she pulled herself through it, frequencies warping around her, fracturing, reassembling. The light turned sharp, painful, beautiful. Every heartbeat, every emotion she'd ever carried surged back into her all at once — joy, sorrow, hunger, fear.

The music shattered.

The world tore open in a burst of color, collapsing in on itself like a wave breaking against the shore. The light dimmed, fading into shadow and rain.

When Nyla opened her eyes, she was lying on the cracked marble of the House's grand hall, rain still falling through the dome. Kian was kneeling beside her, his hands shaking.

Her pulse thrummed against his fingers. Strong. Steady. She took a breath, and the air trembled around her like a plucked string.

He exhaled a ragged laugh. "You came back."

Nyla's eyes glowed faint gold, softer now, but unmistakably alive. "I couldn't leave. The world's too quiet without me."

Tavi's voice echoed from behind a fallen beam. "See? Told you she was too stubborn to stay dead."

Marisol smiled through tears, wiping her face with a shaking hand.

Outside, the first full sunrise broke across the water, and for the first time in centuries, the light didn't burn.

For a long moment, no one said a word. The hall was a ruin of light and shadow — rainwater glimmering across broken marble, the storm's reflection caught in every jagged shard of glass. Steam curled off the wreckage where the bridge's energy had seared through stone.

Tavi was the first to break the silence. "Okay, so… not to ruin the moment, but did anyone else see you *explode into light dust* and then casually respawn like some cosmic remix of yourself? Because I'm not saying I cried, but I definitely cried."

Nyla let out a soft, tired laugh, though it came with a wince. "It wasn't… exactly dying."

Marisol knelt beside her, eyes still wide and glassy. "You disappeared, Nyla. Completely. Your frequency flatlined. Even the scanners stopped reading you. Then the bridge lit up like sunrise and—" she gestured at her, voice breaking, "you were *gone*."

"I was," Nyla said quietly. She brushed a wet strand of hair from her face. "But not the way you think."

Kian watched her carefully. The glow that had once bled from her skin was gone, replaced by something subtler — a pulse under her collarbone, faint but steady, like a heartbeat shared with something much larger. "Where did you go?"

Nyla's gaze drifted upward through the broken dome to the brightening sky. The clouds were thinning now, streaked with gold and violet, the storm's final light. "Somewhere between sound and silence," she said. "It's not a place you can name. More like… a frequency. The one that lives between notes."

Tavi frowned. "I feel like that's not something I should understand, but I'm pretending I do because it sounds really poetic."

Nyla smiled faintly. "That's good enough."

She looked down at her hands. The skin shimmered faintly where raindrops hit it, as if the light beneath her surface hadn't entirely decided to stay hidden. "It was like being inside the music. Everything was vibration — alive, connected. I could feel every Resonant, every heartbeat. It was... infinite. And in the middle of it, I saw her."

Marisol's breath caught. "Ardelia?"

Nyla nodded. "She wasn't the monster I fought. Not there. She was... clear. Like a frequency stripped of all the noise. I think whatever was left of her resonance stayed inside the bridge when I remade it."

Kian frowned, his voice low. "And she spoke to you?"

"She did." Nyla's tone softened. "She told me the bridge needed a guardian — someone to hold it together. That it would collapse without an anchor. I thought that meant staying there. That I had to give up everything to keep the world from falling apart again."

"But you didn't," Marisol said, her voice trembling with awe.

Nyla's smile was faint and sad all at once. "She gave me a choice."

"What kind of choice?" Kian asked.

"To stay and become part of it forever... or return."

Tavi blinked. "And you picked door number 'traumatic resurrection.' Bold choice."

Nyla laughed softly, the sound fragile but real. "It wasn't easy being in that space. It was peace, in its purest form. No hunger. No pain. No division between the

Houses. But peace like that…" she looked around at the broken hall, at the blood, at the friends still standing, "…it's lonely. No sound. No feeling. No growth. Just perfection that never moves."

Kian's voice was barely a whisper. "So, you came back for us."

Her gaze met his. "For *all* of us."

The rain intensified briefly, then softened again, as if the world were exhaling. Nyla tilted her head, listening to the rhythmic drip from the fractured ceiling. "The bridge doesn't need a guardian. It needs resonance. It needs people who are willing to listen, even when it hurts."

Tavi huffed, crossing her arms. "Well, good news — we're definitely hurting."

Marisol cracked a weary smile. "Speak for yourself. I think my ribs started listening about an hour ago."

For a moment, laughter echoed through the ruin, small and trembling but real — the kind of laughter that could only exist after survival.

Nyla sat back, letting it wash over her. The rain fell harder now, drumming a steady rhythm on the marble. She could feel the world humming beneath it — a patchwork of frequencies alive and imperfect and utterly human.

She looked back at them — Kian, Marisol, Tavi — and saw something new in their faces. Not fear. Not awe. Just faith.

Her voice came soft but certain. "Ardelia wasn't wrong about everything. She wanted unity. She just forgot that unity doesn't mean control. It means dissonance that still finds its way back to harmony."

Tavi raised an eyebrow. "You know, for a woman who just came back from the afterlife, you're starting to sound like a motivational poster."

Nyla laughed again, and this time it didn't sound tired. "Maybe that's the point."

Marisol stood, extending a hand to her. "So, Maestra... what now?"

Nyla took it, rising slowly. The storm outside had finally broken for good, the city glinting wet and new beneath the dawn. She turned toward the light, her eyes catching gold again for just a second.

"Now," she said, "we start with the quiet."

Tavi groaned, clutching her side. "I swear, if that's code for more vampire meditation, I'm walking into the sun."

Kian laughed softly, and for the first time since the collapse, Nyla felt the world hum in perfect, imperfect harmony.

# XVIII

Weeks later, the city had found its balance again—or something that almost felt like it. Miami was different now. You could hear it in the air, in the way the breeze off the bay carried a hum that wasn't traffic or neon or ocean. It was life. The resonance shift hadn't ended the Houses, but it had changed them. Some fell apart. Some rebuilt. Some were learning, slowly, that sound could mean more than power.

And at the heart of it all was *Midnight Tempo.*

Once a vampire den hidden under Arista's shadow, now its doors were open. Not just to Resonants or Silents, but to everyone. The sign out front pulsed softly with light that changed with the beat inside, not blood-red anymore, but a deep, warm gold. A pulse that felt like a heartbeat, or maybe a promise.

Inside, the club had been reborn. The walls no longer throbbed with hunger but with rhythm. Speakers lined the ceiling like constellations, glowing faintly with living resonance. The crowd was a strange, beautiful mix—mortals, immortals, House-born and House-forgotten, all moving together to the same song. Some danced. Some just listened. No one fed without consent. No one commanded.

And at the center of it all stood Nyla Voss, Maestra of the House of Sound.

She leaned against the rail of the mezzanine, watching the room below. The light from the stage painted her in gold and blue, faint trails of energy still glowing along her veins. She looked stronger now, but quieter too, like a storm that had learned to be gentle.

Kian stood beside her, half-smiling, a glass of something dark in his hand. "You realize this is chaos, right?"

"Controlled chaos," she said.

He gestured toward the floor. "You've got humans dancing with vampires, Damps running sound for Resonants, and some guy in the corner trying to sell 'spiritual detox tonics' to a group of immortal musicians."

Nyla's lips curved. "Sounds like peace to me."

Marisol crossed the stage below, wearing her usual smirk, gesturing to the tech crew. "Two minutes to live feed," she called. "You ready for your big speech, boss?"

Nyla turned from the balcony, her eyes reflecting the club's glow. "No speeches tonight," she said. "Just music."

Tavi, perched on the bar like it was her throne, raised her drink. "You say that now, but give it five minutes. You've got a Maestra voice. You *love* speeches."

"Not anymore," Nyla said softly. "I used to think sound had to control people. Now I think it just has to reach them."

Kian's smile deepened, small but real. "So, what happens now? The Houses, the Council… all of it?"

She glanced down at the crowd again. "The Houses are still standing, but they're different. They have to be. We're not divided by silence or sound anymore. The old laws broke when the bridge was born. The Council's dissolving, whether they admit it or not. The world's writing its own rhythm now."

He tilted his head. "And what about you?"

"I lead the House of Sound," she said. "But I don't own it. I guide it. Teach it to listen before it speaks. That's what Ardelia never understood."

"She'd hate that."

"She'd also respect it."

The crowd below began to cheer as the lights dimmed and the music faded out. A soft hum filled the space, low and inviting — not the Prime Note, but something reminiscent of it. The bridge, alive and humming through every wire, every pulse.

Nyla descended the steps, the crowd parting instinctively as she crossed to the DJ booth. She rested her palm against the console. It was warm, vibrating faintly under her touch.

Kian joined her. "You feel it too, don't you?"

She nodded. "It's not gone. Just quieter. The bridge still runs through the city—through all of us. We're keeping it alive by living."

Marisol gave the signal from across the room. The lights dimmed further, a single beam illuminating Nyla. She took a deep breath, her fingers finding the sliders on the board.

"This one," she said, voice soft but carrying across the room, "is for everyone who's still learning how to listen."

A familiar bassline rolled through the speakers—smooth, pulsing, impossible to mistake. The first track she ever played at Midnight Tempo, long before any of this had begun.

The crowd erupted.

As the beat built, the floor seemed to pulse with it, each note rippling outward until it reached every heart in the room. Mortals. Vampires. Silents. All moving in the same imperfect rhythm.

Kian stood behind her, his hand resting lightly on her shoulder. "Feels like coming home," he said.

"It is," Nyla replied.

She closed her eyes. The bass deepened, and for a split second, she felt it — that hum beneath her skin, the whisper of light that had lived within her ever since she chose to return. It wasn't calling her away this time. It was answering.

The bridge pulsed faintly through her veins, reminding her of what she was — and what she'd become. Not a weapon. Not a god. A conductor.

For the first time in centuries, the Houses weren't ruled by silence or fear. They were ruled by song.

The night stretched on, a symphony of heartbeats and sound.

And when the final note trembled through the floor, soft and infinite, Nyla smiled—not because it was perfect, but because it wasn't.

Because it was *alive.*

Outside, Miami glowed against the water, the city's heartbeat syncing once more to its own imperfect, beautiful sound.

The song spilled into the street, where the wet pavement glowed with reflected light. People gathered outside the open doors of *Midnight Tempo,* drawn not by curiosity, but by resonance — that faint, living vibration that whispered in their bones.

It wasn't just music anymore. It was connection.

The bass rolled through the city blocks, bouncing off glass towers and slipping down alleyways. It reached the waterfront, where the moon trembled across the bay. It reached the old industrial district, where the House of Smoke once thrived behind shuttered doors and whispered illusions.

Inside one of those buildings, a man sat at a long table surrounded by flickering holograms—remnants of Smoke's illusions that hadn't yet faded since the resonance shift. They used to respond to command. Now, they danced on their own.

The man's name was Lucien Ola, interim head of the House of Smoke. His once-perfect suit was wrinkled, his dark hair falling loose over tired eyes. A cigarette burned down between his fingers, forgotten.

He watched the illusions flicker: echoes of faces long gone, flickering in and out of existence with each bassline that pulsed through the floor. The walls of the old House were vibrating softly, as though even they had decided to remember what truth felt like.

"Still hearing her?" a voice asked from the shadows.

Lucien didn't look up. "You can't *not* hear her."

A woman stepped into the light—slender, sharp-eyed, dressed in the metallic silks favored by the House of Stone. Her name was Yara Idris, Stone's liaison, though lately the word "House" meant less and less.

"She's changing everything," Yara said.

Lucien smirked faintly. "Good. The world needed a little distortion."

Yara studied him. "And the Houses?"

"They'll adapt," he said, though his voice lacked conviction. He gestured toward the vibrating walls, toward the illusions that now flickered in time with Nyla's rhythm. "They're already learning to breathe again. For the first time in a century, Smoke's visions aren't lies. They're… memories."

Yara frowned. "That sounds dangerous."

"Truth usually is."

He stubbed out his cigarette, stood, and looked toward the window. The sound from *Midnight Tempo* carried across the city like a heartbeat, muffled but undeniable. "Tell your Maestra in Stone she's not the only one rebuilding," he said. "And tell her—" he hesitated, the faintest ghost of a smile playing at his lips, "—if she sees Nyla Voss before I do, I still owe her a dance."

Yara arched a brow. "You think she'd accept it?"

Lucien laughed softly, bitter and fond. "Only if she leads."

The sound of it lingered in the room long after his smile faded. Smoke curled from the extinguished cigarette, spiraling toward the ceiling where the light flickered in rhythmic sync with the distant bass rolling across the city. The whole building pulsed faintly now — the way it used to, back when illusion and hunger kept the House of Smoke alive. But this was different. There was no command to it, no artifice. The resonance wasn't obeying anyone. It was *responding.*

He crossed to the window, pushing open the warped frame. Rain-scented air drifted in, cool and alive. From here, the city looked like veins of light— gold, white, and amber — threading through the dark. And beneath it, faint but undeniable, came the rhythm from the waterfront.

The sound wasn't loud, but it was constant. The bassline echoed through the concrete, crawling up the walls until Lucien could feel it vibrating in his ribs. Every few seconds, the old illusions around him shimmered—a thousand echoes of past versions of himself, flickering in and out with every beat. One smiled; one frowned; one vanished before he could tell which was real.

He had spent a century perfecting control—of image, of sound, of truth—and now the city hummed to someone else's rhythm.

He didn't hate it.

Yara watched him, arms crossed. "You could join them, you know. Whatever she's building, it's bigger than Sound now."

Lucien tilted his head, listening as the beat changed tempo—soft, then sharper, then fading into a syncopated rhythm that felt like an invitation. "No," he said finally. "I'll let her have the spotlight. Smoke's work is quieter."

Yara smiled faintly. "Still scheming?"

"Always." He reached for another cigarette, lit it, and took a slow drag. The ember burned gold instead of red, catching the light like a heartbeat. "But maybe I'll send a message. Something subtle. Something she'll feel."

He turned back toward the window, toward the hum that stitched the skyline together. "The world doesn't know it yet," he said, "but she didn't end the Houses. She just rewrote the song."

A single drop of rain slipped down the glass, tracing a line that caught the flicker of neon from the street below. Lucien followed its path, then closed his eyes as the next beat from *Midnight Tempo* hit — deeper this time, brighter.

The pulse rippled through the city, into every structure still standing. In the House of Stone, chandeliers vibrated faintly. In the underground halls of Silence, the air pressure shifted just enough to make the walls sigh. And somewhere in the ruins of Sound's first cathedral, a shattered console blinked to life, its speakers humming a single note that wasn't supposed to exist anymore.

Lucien smiled, smoke curling past his lips. "There she is," he murmured.

Back at *Midnight Tempo,* the song built toward its final measure.

Nyla stood behind the console, her hand hovering above the controls as she watched the crowd. Vampires and humans danced side by side — laughter spilling, tears shining, frequencies blending. She could feel the hum running through them all, the bridge alive in every motion.

Kian leaned close, his voice barely audible over the sound. "You realize this isn't just a club anymore."

She nodded. "It's a frequency. A home. Maybe even a prayer."

"Careful," he said, smiling faintly. "You're starting to sound like a Maestra."

She met his gaze, warmth flickering behind her eyes. "I am a Maestra. Just not the kind they used to make."

The bass deepened one last time; a slow, grounding note that filled the entire room with light. The crowd stopped dancing and simply *listened*.

Outside, across the city, the vibration carried. Through the House of Smoke, through the iron-clad walls of Stone, through the quiet sanctums of Silence, and even into the abandoned recording rooms where Sound had once divided its own.

The music wasn't asking for allegiance anymore. It was asking for unity.

Nyla closed her eyes and let the last note fade.

The room didn't erupt into applause. It didn't need to. The quiet that followed was fuller than any cheer could be.

Marisol, leaning against the wall, exhaled softly. "You did it."

Nyla smiled, her voice barely a whisper. "No. *We* did."

Tavi raised her glass from the bar. "I vote we call this the post-apocalyptic afterparty and never talk about the part where we almost died again."

Nyla laughed, the sound bright and unguarded. "Agreed."

Kian reached for her hand, his thumb brushing across her wrist where her pulse still hummed with gold. "You can rest now," he said.

She shook her head gently, her gaze lifting toward the ceiling, toward the open sky that pulsed faintly with reflected city light. "The world's still tuning itself," she said. "I'm just making sure it stays in key."

Outside, the night deepened. Miami glowed gold against the water — a city reborn, humming in harmony.

And somewhere across that light, in an old building where smoke and illusions still danced, Lucien Vale smiled as he lifted his glass toward the horizon.

"To the Maestra who broke the silence," he murmured.

As the bassline rolled through the city once more, every seemed to pause for the briefest moment, listening to the same song.

The world was changing, and Nyla Voss was still conducting.

# Author's Note

When I started writing *Midnight Tempo,* I knew I wanted to do something a little different with the vampire genre—something charged, kinetic, and alive. Vampires have been written every which way: tragic lovers, cursed immortals, glittering antiheroes. But what I wanted was *energy*—a story that pulsed like a heartbeat under neon lights, that felt as alive and hungry as the city itself. I wanted a vampire story that *moved.*

Setting it in Miami felt natural. It's a place that hums with contradictions—heat and glamour, sin and salvation, music and silence. There's a rhythm to that city, a kind of living heartbeat that never really stops, even when the night ends. I wanted readers to *hear* it through Nyla: every bass drop, every echo of desire, every dangerous note she rides between power and vulnerability.

From the start, I also knew Nyla had to be the kind of protagonist we rarely see in this space—a plus-sized, Black woman who owns every inch of her presence. Not the sidekick. Not the comic relief. Not the friend hyping someone else's story. She *is* the story. She's confident, magnetic, complicated, and flawed in ways that make her real. She's not "powerful in spite of" her body—her body is part of her power.

As a plus-sized Black woman myself, I'm tired of stories where we're the punchline or the stereotype. I wanted to create a heroine who didn't apologize for taking up space, who could be sensual and commanding without being softened or diminished. Nyla doesn't just walk into a room—she takes over the frequency.

*Midnight Tempo* is my love letter to that kind of unapologetic existence. To the women who've been told they're "too much," "too loud," or "too visible." To the ones who learned to find beauty in their own chaos and rhythm in their own skin.

If you felt the bassline of this story in your chest—if it made you want to move, to feel, to *own* your volume—then it did what it was meant to.

Here's to more stories that sing in new frequencies. And to every woman who's ever been told to turn herself down—may you keep the volume up.

# Stay Connected

Hey there, amazing reader!

I hope you enjoyed diving into my world of stories as much as I loved creating them! Your thoughts and feedback mean everything to me, and I'd love to hear what you think. Whether it's a review, a favorite quote, or just a quick "OMG, I need more!"—I'm all ears!

**Your Reviews Matter!** If you loved what you just read (or even if you have thoughts on how it made you feel), leaving a review helps more readers discover my books. Plus, it totally makes my day!

Let's stay connected! Follow me, tag me, and send me a message—I love chatting with fellow book lovers!

**Blog:** MyuniqueGreen.com
**Instagram: @_cmajor_**
**Snapchat:** Cece_major

Can't wait to hear from you! Until next time—keep turning those pages!

# About Myunique

Myunique C. Green is a versatile and celebrated author whose work spans across genres, including mystery, thriller, young adult fiction, dystopian science fiction, and personal memoir. Based in Houston, Texas, she began her literary journey with the independently published *Bloodlines: Everything That Glitter* in 2012, which climbed to the Top 10 on Amazon Kindle's Bestseller list. Since then, she has continued to captivate readers with her unique voice and compelling storytelling.

Her titles, such as *713*, a chart-topping mystery short story, and *Grand Rising*, a dystopian epic, showcase her ability to explore complex themes and engage audiences with fresh perspectives. Myunique's deeply personal memoir, *To Mend a Broken Heart*, stands out as a powerful testament to resilience and healing, inspiring readers with her honesty and courage.

Known for her innovative approach and emotional depth, Myunique's writing reflects her passion for tackling challenging narratives that resonate with readers on both an emotional and intellectual level. She has received accolades for her work, including an award from the Midtown Journal for her short fiction.

When she's not writing, Myunique is a dedicated teacher, student, and parent, continually pushing boundaries and inspiring others to find strength in their own stories. Through her work, she strives to connect with readers, leaving a lasting impression of hope, resilience, and the power of storytelling.

Excerpt From

# HEATFALL

Cinderpath didn't so much join the festival as claim space within it. They moved through the southern edge in a surge—wagon doors flung open before the wheels stopped, music clashing with the steady beat of Crimson Wake's drums. Their banners were faded and mismatched, but there was a certain audacity in that, a statement that polish was for caravans who had time to stand still.

Tessa saw him before he saw her.

Cael dismounted from his frost-ox in one fluid motion, his boots hitting the ground with the easy balance of someone who'd spent his life moving. Broad-shouldered, long-limbed, his coat hung open enough to show the worn leather harness across his chest—maps rolled tight in one loop, a compass the size of her palm hanging in another. The firelight burnished his skin into deep bronze, throwing copper sparks through the braids worked into his hair.

And gods help her, her pulse jumped. She wasn't sure if it was relief that he was alive, or the kind of anger that wanted to come with teeth.

When his gaze finally swept to her, his smile came slow, like he'd just stumbled across an old map he'd forgotten he owned.

He started toward her without hesitation, threading through the crowd with the same unhurried confidence he'd worn the first time they met—years before the frostfront and bad decisions had carved a canyon between them.

"Tessa," he said, voice warm, as if her name had been sitting on his tongue for months instead of years. "Didn't think you'd mind me dropping by. Thought you might even miss me."

Her lips stayed in a line that could cut. "You called this meeting," she said, not asking, just naming it for what it was.

He gave a half-shrug, the motion loose. "Someone had to. The frost's closing faster this year. Another week without shifting routes, and you'd be counting bodies."

She stepped closer, just enough to make him stop moving toward her. "Don't act like you've done me a favor."

His grin didn't falter, but his eyes flickered—just for a second—to something sharper. "Three years is a long time to stay mad."

"And three years is a long time to pretend you don't know why."

Around them, the difference between their caravans unfolded in the space of a glance. Crimson Wake's lines stayed tight and orderly, crimson banners swaying in measured arcs above neatly staked tents. Cinderpath sprawled in loose clusters, their wagons in a rough semicircle, fires already lit and food cooking in mismatched pots. One caravan moved like a blade, the other like a tide—neither wrong, both dangerous.

She could feel the heat from the First Flame at her back, the night pressing in around them, the noise of their people folding into one another. She knew if she let herself say more, she'd see red, and there were too many eyes here for that.

"Enjoy the fire," she said instead, turning on her heel before he could answer.

Behind her, she thought she heard him chuckle—low, amused, and utterly infuriating.

Tessa didn't look back, but she felt his presence at the edge of her awareness, the way a storm sits just beyond the horizon—close enough to smell, impossible to ignore.

The festival swelled around them, firelight bending over bodies in motion. Traders from visiting caravans wove through the crowd, hawking their wares—spools of copper wire scavenged from the bones of frostbitten cities, vials of thawed berry wine, polished stones that still held the faintest trace of summer warmth. The air pulsed with overlapping rhythms—Crimson Wake's drums steady and measured, Cinderpath's percussion breaking in syncopated bursts, daring anyone to follow.

Her Shields tracked the newcomers, hands never straying far from their weapons, though their expressions stayed neutral. That was the unspoken rule—look like you're enjoying yourself, but keep counting exits.

From the southern quarter, Cinderpath had already thrown up makeshift stalls: wooden planks balanced on barrels, the surfaces crowded with salvaged tools, frost-resistant hides, even a handful of heat-stones chipped and imperfect. Their people moved like they owned the space, bartering without apology, laughing too loudly, spilling drink where Crimson Wake's merchants would have poured with care.

The contrast was more than style—it was survival philosophy. Crimson Wake's order meant predictability, predictability meant trust in trade. Cinderpath's chaos meant adaptability, and adaptability could save your life when frost rolled in early.

Venn, the Heart of Crimson Wake, appeared at her side with a clay mug in each hand. "Thought you might want something to take the edge off," he said, passing one to her.

She took it, the spiced wine's heat sinking into her fingers before it reached her lips. "I'd rather keep the edge for now."

His gaze followed hers toward the southern quarter. "He's already spoken to three other Leads tonight. Whatever he's here for, it's more than the pleasure of your company."

Tessa's mouth curved—half-smile, half-threat. "I'm well aware."

They both turned at the same moment toward the outer ring where a messenger from Cinderpath stood on the edge of the firelight, scanning for her. He was young, bareheaded despite the chill, his coat marked with Cinderpath's scavenger sigil—a sun half-buried in frost. When he caught her eye, he tipped his chin toward the ridge where the caravans' Leads traditionally met in private.

Venn sighed. "You're going up there, aren't you?"

"If I don't, he'll just come down here and make a scene." She drained the wine, handed back the cup, and started toward the ridge.

The climb was short, but the view from the top stretched across the entire Copper Vale, the fire below flickering in a sea of red, gold, and mismatched colors. Cael was waiting, leaning against one of the frost-slick boulders, arms folded like this was a casual meeting and not the first time they'd stood this close in three years.

"You came," he said, like it was a small victory.

"You summoned me," she replied.

His grin widened. "Sounds better when you say it."

She stopped just out of arm's reach. "Say what you came to say."

He tilted his head toward the distant dark beyond the ridge. "Signal came through the network two nights ago. One of the Accord stations is still active. Coordinates are moving, but right now they're buried deep in frostfront territory."

Her pulse stilled for a moment, not from fear but from the calculation already running in her head. Accord stations were myths to most caravans—legends of old-world tech that could predict weather, maybe even shift it.

"If you're telling me this," she said slowly, "it's because you want something."

He shrugged like it was the most natural thing in the world. "Neither of us can reach it alone. But together? We've got a shot. You know I'm right."

Tessa looked at him hard, searching for the tell she used to know—the flicker at the corner of his mouth, the shift of his weight when he was hiding something. The years had changed him. Broadened him. Sharpened him. But that same restless light was still there in his eyes, and it was dangerous.

"You think I've forgotten the last time we trusted each other?" she asked.

"No," he said, voice low now. "I think you've been trying to."

The drums from below carried up the ridge, steady in the dark. The firelight reached them in thin, wavering threads. And between them, the cold air seemed sharper than it had a moment ago.

Tessa didn't answer right away. The wind off the ridge carried the bite of ice, sliding down the back of her neck despite the firelight below.

Accord stations.

For a heartbeat, the present bled into memory—her father's tent when she was a girl, the canvas walls lined with curling maps printed on sheets so thin the edges tore if you breathed too hard. The emblem of the Atmospheric Accord stamped in the corner: a circle split into four, each quadrant painted in the colors of the seasons that no longer existed. Spring green, summer gold, autumn red, winter blue.

She remembered kneeling on the furs beside him as his callused fingers traced arcs across the paper—heat currents drawn in orange, frostfront flows in pale blue, the wide band of summer sweeping across continents in a predictable loop. Back then, the stations spoke to each other in a constant hum, sending warnings days in advance, plotting courses for ships and caravans before either had to change direction.

Her father would point to their place on the map, his voice certain. *As long as we can read these lines, we'll always find summer.*

But after the Shattering, the lines broke. Stations went silent. Maps became artifacts. And now—if Cael was telling the truth—one of those stations was still breathing.

The memory snapped like thread, and she was back on the ridge, Cael watching her with the faintest glint of satisfaction, like he knew exactly where her mind had gone.

"You can read them," he said. Not a question.

Her jaw tightened. "If the tech's still intact."

"Then you see why I came to you." His grin tilted again, that mix of charm and provocation that had always made her want to either kiss him or strike him. "No one else can do this."

She looked past him, into the dark where frost swallowed the land, thinking of those old lines her father once traced and how many lives they'd saved. And how many more they could.

Tessa let the silence stretch, the drums from the vale below filling the space between them. "You've got nerve showing up here with this," she said at last. "You vanish for three years, and now I'm supposed to believe you've stumbled across a miracle and just… need my help?"

Cael didn't flinch. "Not a miracle. A fact. And yes, I need your help. You need mine, too—whether you want to admit it or not."

Her laugh was short and sharp, without humor. "You overestimate your importance."

“No,” he said, stepping in just enough for the cold to rise between them like another presence. “I know exactly how important I am to this. You’ve seen frost move fast before—this year it’s faster. Without that station’s data, without a change in the route, you’re going to lose people.”

She folded her arms, the leather of her coat creaking. “I’ve kept Crimson Wake alive without you. I’ll keep doing it.”

“You’ll keep bleeding for it,” he countered, his tone still infuriatingly even. “I’m not here to take over, Tessa. I’m here because if either of us tries this alone, the frost gets what it’s wanted all along.”

Her eyes narrowed. “And what’s that?”

He gave the faintest smile. “Everything.”

The way he said it—quiet, certain—pulled at something she didn’t want touched. She turned away, looking out over the vast dark. The frostfront wasn’t visible yet, but she imagined it out there: a slow-moving wall swallowing forests, cities, entire histories without pause.

She hated that he was right about the danger. Hated more that he thought that gave him the upper hand.

“If I say no?” she asked.

“You won’t,” he said. Not arrogant—just sure. “Because you care about your people more than you care about hating me.”

Her jaw tightened until she thought it might crack. “You’re still the same. Still certain the world bends if you stand in the right place.”

"And you're still the same," he replied, "pretending you don't want to be the one steering it."

She forced herself to step back before she started seeing red. "Enjoy the festival, Cael. My answer isn't tonight."

His grin returned, slow and needling. "I'll be here when you change your mind."

She left him on the ridge, the firelight from below painting his silhouette against the cold.

The noise of the festival swelled as Tessa descended from the ridge, each step drawing her back into the heat and color below. The First Flame roared at the center of the vale, its light catching on a hundred moving faces—Crimson Wake's disciplined lines blurring under the crush of visitors, Cinderpath's looser knots of people spilling laughter and drink wherever they went.

The moment she stepped off the last slope, Venn was at her side again, eyes searching her face for whatever she'd just carried down from that meeting. She didn't offer it. Instead, she scanned the crowd the way she always did—by function, not by face. Shields still patrolled the perimeter, their routes tight. The cooks kept the stew lines moving. Traders were doing brisk business, though she noticed more Cinderpath coin changing hands than Crimson Wake's.

Cinderpath had claimed the southern quarter like they'd been invited to it, their wagons pulled in wide arcs that made the space look more like a street market than a camp. Smoke from their fire pits rose thick with the scent of seared meat, sharper than the stew and bread of Crimson Wake's ring. Music spilled from their corner too—faster, rougher, the kind that made people dance in tight circles until they were breathless.

The differences between them were impossible to miss. Where Crimson Wake tents were lined in disciplined rows, stakes driven flush, Cinderpath's shelters stood at odd angles, half the doors open to the night. Where Crimson Wake traders counted coins before passing goods, Cinderpath bartered with laughter and handshakes, sending goods on before payment was even clear.

Her people noticed. She caught the sideways glances from her merchants as a group of Cinderpath hunters swaggered past with new gear bought in bulk. She saw Jorn's mouth tighten as two of their younger scouts leaned in toward the music, curious.

"Your people are watching," Venn murmured.

"They always are," she said.

On the far side of the fire, Cael was in the thick of his own caravan, a knot of them gathered around as he spoke. His posture was loose, easy, but she could tell he was working them—just as he'd worked her on the ridge. Whatever he was saying had them laughing, nodding, clapping him on the back. He hadn't so much entered Crimson Wake's ground as folded it around himself, making the place his.

Tessa's fingers curled at her sides, the warmth from the fire seeping into her skin but not loosening the knot in her chest. He was alive, and that still meant something to her, though she didn't know if that something was gratitude or fury.

When one of Cinderpath's traders—young, grinning, oblivious—offered her a mug of whatever they were brewing in that corner, she shook her head once and moved on.

Let them think she was keeping her distance for politics' sake. The truth was, she wasn't ready to find out if her heart skipped because of him… or in spite of him.

# OTHER BOOKS

Available in Digital & Paperback

**Young Adult Fantasy**
Everything That Glitters (Bloodlines Book 1)
Dead to Rights (Bloodlines Book 2)
Awakened (The Reignmere Chronicles Book 1)
Reaping 101

**Sci-Fi & Dystopian**
Cipher (Hybrid Horizons Book 1)
Talia (Hybrid Horizons Book 2)
Grand Rising
Zombies Anonymous
Heatfall

**Literature & Fiction**
Psinder
Hysteria
Linked By Ink (Available as Audiobook)
Hearts, Hype & Other Hoaxes

**Women's Non-Fiction**
The C is for Complex
To Mend a Broken Heart (Available as Audiobook)
Sweet Savage
Girl, It Hasn't Happened Yet!
Love Letters to Heaven

**Mystery & Suspense**
Chopped & Skrewed (Available as Audiobook)
Last Seen (Available as Audiobook)
Compulsive
Anywhere But Here
By Her Blood

www.ingramcontent.com/pod-product-compliance
Lightning Source LLC
LaVergne TN
LVHW091041080826
845145LV00002B/578

* 9 7 8 1 1 0 5 9 5 8 8 4 7 *